Stratford Brunswick cannot believe that Baron von Lunenburg has identified as the woman on whom he will focus his unsavory attentions.

Stratford followed Lunenburg's glance to an arched entryway on the far side of the room. The woman was wearing a blue gown, and her light hair was curled into ringlets on either side of her face, a style that had become popular in recent years. Most of her hair was covered by a broad ribbon in the same color that had some sort of proper name, one he couldn't remember.

But when she turned her face toward the fire, he saw those blue eyes and lips as pink as a spring rose. Stratford nearly dropped his glass of lemonade. "Her? That is the one?"

"Indeed." Lunenburg smiled, then took another swig of his drink.

Jealousy returned with a vengeance. Stratford tried to put on an appearance of maintaining his composure by drawing himself up to his full height and taking in a breath. "She is new here, is she not?"

"You should be more privy to that knowledge than I, since you have been a lifelong resident here." The baron smiled with the expression of one who held the key to secret knowledge. "I know. I am a sore winner. I should not tease you in such a manner. Of course you do not know her. That, my friend, is Lady Dorothea Witherspoon, Helen's cousin visiting from London."

Lady Dorothea Witherspoon from London. So that was the identity of his mystery woman.

"Lovely, is she not?" Lunenburg prompted.

Too lovely for you.

TAMELA HANCOCK MURRAY is an award-winning, best-selling author. *Journeys* is her tenth title written for Heartsong Presents. She is also the author of six novellas and seven Bible trivia books. When not writing, Tamela enjoys time spent with her wonderful husband and daughters. She also enjoys Beth Moore Bible studies as a member of "Beth's Buds" at her church. Tamela hopes that her stories of God-centered romance edify and entertain her sisters in Christ. Contact Tamela by e-mailing her at Tamela@tamelahancockmurray.com. Visit her web site at www.tamelahancockmurray.com.

Books by Tamela Hancock Murray

HEARTSONG PRESENTS
HP213—Picture of Love
HP408—Destinations
HP453—The Elusive Mr. Perfect
HP501—Thrill of the Hunt
HP544—A Light among Shadows
HP568—Loveswept
HP598—More Than Friends
HP616—The Lady and the Cad
HP639—Love's Denial

Don't miss out on any of our super romances. Write to us at the following address for information on our newest releases and club information.

Heartsong Presents Readers' Service
PO Box 721
Uhrichsville, OH 44683

Or visit www.heartsongpresents.com

Journeys

Tamela Hancock Murray

Heartsong Presents

To Jill,
my daughter
who is about to embark on her own journey.

A note from the Author:
I love to hear from my readers! You may correspond with me by writing:

Tamela Hancock Murray
Author Relations
PO Box 719
Uhrichsville, OH 44683

ISBN 1-59310-788-9

JOURNEYS

All scripture quotations are taken from the King James Version of the Bible.

All of the characters and events in this book are fictitious. Any resemblance to actual persons, living or dead, or to actual events is purely coincidental.

Our mission is to publish and distribute inspirational products offering exceptional value and biblical encouragement to the masses.

PRINTED IN THE U.S.A.

one

"*Newgate. That is precisely where you will go if you are not able to settle your accounts with due haste. I managed to hold off your creditors until after Christmas, but since the advent of the new year, they want their money. Now.*"

Her solicitor's words rang through Lady Dorothea Witherspoon's mind. She shuddered at the thought of the wretched conditions she would be forced to endure in debtor's prison if she did not somehow convince her cousin to let her borrow a small fortune, ten thousand pounds. The thought of having to beg a distant relative she barely knew left her stomach in a knot.

She decided to concentrate instead on the bold music she heard playing in the nearby ballroom of her cousin's country estate. Yet the merry tune and jovial voices of Helen's guests did little to cheer her. She inhaled the delicious scent of hot apple cider seasoned with cinnamon. Dorothea imagined herself partaking of a cup, warming her body and soul. Had she been hungry, aromas of meat pies and sugary pastries would have been tempting, for pleasant fragrances told Dorothea that Helen obviously had set out a feast for her guests. Surely a cousin who could host such extravagance could find a way to help Dorothea when her need was so great.

Heavenly Father, please allow Helen to let me have the money. If she chooses not to offer me any assistance, I have no notion where to turn.

Dorothea hadn't meant to arrive in the midst of a party, but the delay of her journey by coach couldn't be helped. Thankfully she was wearing her best traveling suit. The rented coach had stopped at an inn in the village to allow the passengers to rejuvenate themselves. As a result, Dorothea's assurance that she appeared fresh gave her enough fortitude to assure that strangers wouldn't know how much her back hurt or that her muscles still felt tight from the long and bumpy trip to the country from London.

"I will make my excuses, have Helen show me to my quarters, and retire," she muttered.

Dorothea felt a gaze upon her. She looked in the direction of the ballroom doorway to the west and spied a tall man standing with posture erect, as though he felt proud of his stature. In spite of his distance from her, the force of his presence emanated across the expansive foyer to where she stood. His notice of her made her feel shy; she made a point of noticing the potted plant next to a mahogany occasional table.

She could still feel him studying her, so she returned his interest. Inquisitive eyes peered back at her and fit well with his strong, manly features that she found quite appealing to view. His form was apparent, backlit from party lights. A dark waistcoat hugged his masculine chest and showed off a trim middle. His glance locked with hers for an instant, just long enough to express interest. In the demure manner of a lady, she drank in a glimpse of his handsome countenance and dark wavy hair, then averted her eyes to study dancing flames in the fireplace. Perhaps she could summon the strength to make an appearance at the festivities after all.

Her admirer slipped back into the crowd when Helen, dressed in a stylish gown fashioned of green silk, bounded into the foyer. "Dorothea. I am so glad you are finally here. I was anticipating your arrival late yesterday."

"Good evening, Helen. I thought you might greet me in French. I have been brushing up on the language just so we could converse."

Helen's laugh echoed against the tall corners of the room. "Now that I am a mother, I have overcome my girlish urge to follow the trend of speaking French. In fact, you will find little French spoken here at all anymore. My friends and I found such pomposity amusing for a time, but no longer."

Dorothea couldn't express disappointment at such an announcement. She ventured onto safe conversational territory. "How is your little girl?"

"Very sweet."

&

Helen chattered on about herself and her immediate concerns, not bothering to ask Dorothea much about herself or the purpose of her visit. She surmised that if the butler hadn't taken her winter coat and hat, she would still be wearing her outer garments throughout Helen's monologue.

As was her nature, Dorothea could find an excuse for Helen. From a closer relation, Dorothea would have expected an immediate embrace, but she hadn't seen Helen in more than a decade, and her cousin's vain nature had demonstrated itself in her self-absorbed letters. The lack of warmth didn't surprise her.

"I am so sorry for any inconvenience I have caused you," Dorothea apologized after Helen spent herself on the litany. "I certainly never would have timed my arrival for the midst of a party. Icy rains slowed the progress of our coach."

"I suspected as much. We have been experiencing our share of inclement weather this week. Well, no one can help the rain. How could I not forgive a cousin I have not seen in so long?" Helen looked into her face. "Yes, I would recognize you anywhere. Those blue eyes are as striking as ever. And your hair has not darkened a bit with age. Still as bright a blond as ever."

"And you are even more beautiful than the young woman you were—the woman I always envied," Dorothea said.

And still do.

How fortunate Helen was not to have a care in the world. She was married to a man she loved, and she had given birth to a healthy girl in the autumn of 1815. All that, and they were wealthy. Wealthy enough never to worry. They didn't have a father who cared so little about them that he gambled away their rightful inheritance.

Only after Father's death had Dorothea discovered her plight. To Dorothea's mind, his creditors weren't playing fair to demand payment from his estate, but they did—the exceptions being only two merchants who were fond friends of her family. The other men, mainly unsavory proprietors of gaming establishments, held their palms out for prompt payment almost as soon as her father's casket was forever closed. They cared not a whit about her plight. They only demanded their money.

After the initial shock waned, she made every effort to satisfy Father's creditors. She sold her London home, where she had spent happy childhood years oblivious to her parents' problems. Desperate, she sold her jewels, china, silver, and other family heirlooms. Such items were but earthly trinkets, yet they were meant to be passed to her own children and grandchildren. The people who bought them were pleased enough with their bargains gained from the forced sale. Dorothea was certain they wouldn't appreciate them nearly as much as her heirs would have. Even then, the turmoil hadn't seemed worth the effort. The money raised still proved insufficient. Her mother would be heartbroken if she knew her treasures had ended up in the hands of unsentimental strangers, and insulted if she could have witnessed how Dorothea had been forced to part with many of her possessions for a fraction of their worth.

She needed more money. Ten thousand pounds, to be exact. And it was all her father's fault. Why had he been so reckless?

For the hundredth time, Dorothea reminded herself that bitterness toward her father would do no good and would displease the Lord. After all, the only reason he had been so careless was because his heart had been broken over her dear mother's death.

Whether as a loan or gift, Dorothea didn't care what terms Helen asked regarding the money as long as she could settle her debts until she could decide how to proceed with the rest of her life—a life that had suddenly changed in its expectations.

"You envied me?" Helen waved her fan more to proclaim her slight embarrassment at being complimented than to cool herself against a winter's night. "Ah, but no doubt all the girls your age envy you. Surely now that you are out of mourning you will be the center of attention at every social occasion."

Dorothea was just about to object when she remembered the mystery man. "I do enjoy socials."

"Good." Helen tilted her head toward the party. "Do change out of that traveling suit and into a gown. You must join the birthday celebration."

"Ah, so this is a birthday celebration."

"Yes, in honor of Baron Hans von Lunenburg."

"Oh." Judging from Helen's look, she expected Dorothea to know the guest of honor. "I do not believe I have had the pleasure of meeting him. I do not suppose he is a dark-haired gentleman wearing a fine blue suit?"

"Why would you think that?"

"I just saw someone standing in the doorway." Dorothea tilted her head to where the handsome man had been.

"Actually, Baron von Lunenburg has light brown hair and a mustache, so he must not be the one you saw."

"This man was about thirty and tall and trim."

Helen thought for a moment. "That sounds like Lord Stratford Brunswick."

"Lord Stratford Brunswick." A name of dignity and style that sounded distinctive as it rolled off her tongue.

Helen shrugged. "His pedigree is acceptable but minor."

Dorothea resisted the urge to remind Helen that a baron was one of the lower-ranking members of the European aristocracy. "There is more to a person than pedigree."

"To a poor woman, yes. But remember, you are a Witherspoon."

Dorothea tried not to flinch. Helen still didn't know the

damage Father had done to the Witherspoon name and that at this point in time many of her privileged and wealthy peers would consider her poor. She dreaded her anticipated request doubly.

"So," Helen ventured, "I assume your visit here is more than just to renew old family ties?"

Dorothea's throat tightened. Had Helen indeed already heard about her father's penchant for gambling? She swallowed and took a breath. "What do you mean?"

Helen cocked her head and regarded her through slyly slitted eyes. "You have come here to find a husband?"

Dorothea didn't know whether to laugh or to feel more nervous. Marriage wasn't without appeal. But she could offer no dowry. Rather, she would be a drain on a new husband's coffers. Who would consider her?

No one.

She cleared her throat. "Finding a husband is not on my mind in the least. I—I have other affairs to tend to that are far more pressing at the moment."

Helen fanned her face with renewed vigor. "What do you mean?"

Dorothea couldn't speak. She looked at the points of her kid leather boots, fashioned for her during better times. From the corner of her eye, she noticed a few stragglers had wandered into the area by the ballroom to watch the flames flicker in the fireplace. Whereas Helen and Dorothea had been able to speak in privacy before, the guests' presence meant they could now be overheard.

"Come." Helen took her by the arm. "Let us go into the study." She motioned at a nearby manservant. "Take Lady Witherspoon's baggage to her quarters. The Elizabeth Room on the east wing."

"Yes, milady." He hurried to obey.

Helen glanced at the grandfather clock positioned near the fireplace. "I shall show you to your bedchamber with haste after we speak in the study," Helen told her. "I have only a few moments. Certainly my guests have noticed my absence by now."

"I can wait."

"But I cannot." Concern colored her face, a fact that relieved Dorothea. Perhaps Helen was prone to compassion after all.

She followed Helen upstairs to the study. On the way Dorothea noticed portraits of ancestors hanging in the large hallways. Some she recognized as ancestors she shared with Helen. Others she assumed were related to Helen's mother—people with whom she wasn't familiar since she and Helen were related through their fathers—or members of the Syms lineage. A painter herself, she noticed the fine brushstrokes and how the eyes of the subjects seemed to follow her as she walked, both signs that the muses had commissioned superior artists. The portraits showed their subjects dressed in the most fashionable and fine garments of their time in history. Surely Helen had made an equal match in lineage and wealth.

The study was no disappointment in luxury or comfort despite the fact that the fire had died. Judging from the placement of two desks and matching bookcases on opposite sides of the room, Helen and Luke shared it. Dorothea wondered why, since the house was large enough that such sharing shouldn't have been necessary. Dorothea imagined they enjoyed working together in close proximity. The thought of such a happy marriage panged her heart with unwanted envy.

Heavenly Father, forgive me.

Dorothea took one of the seats in front of Helen's desk, a petite model carved in an elaborate fashion. Helen sat in the one across from her.

"Now that we are alone, you can feel free to be candid. I need to know, what is the real reason for your visit?"

"I have a request. I'm afraid it is not a small one." Dorothea swallowed and wondered if Helen would demand that she leave hardly before she had entered. The prospect of venturing back out into the frigid evening just so she could find a room for the night at the local inn held little attraction. More importantly, minor pedigree or not, she wanted to meet Lord Stratford Brunswick before she left.

"What is it? I do not have an indeterminate period here." The edge in Helen's voice left her feeling even uneasier.

Dorothea wasn't sure where to begin, so she jumped in with both feet but with the dread of one taking a dare to swim the filthy Thames River. "I am sure you can imagine how the deaths of my parents have changed my circumstances."

Helen tapped her foot. "Of course. I know losing both parents so unexpectedly has been a hardship for you."

"Yes. I miss them both terribly. Especially dear Mother."

"But at least you are well equipped to find a husband. I assume my uncle left you with plenty of money to offer suitors a handsome dowry—one large enough to impress even worldly gentlemen in London."

"Regrettably, my situation is not quite as comfortable as you imagined."

"Really?" Dorothea could see that Helen's shock was genuine. "Why not?"

"I suppose you heard how heartbroken Father was after Mother's death."

"Yes, I did."

"He took her death to heart. Blamed himself for it, really. I would often hear him lament that if only he had not insisted on taking her on that trip abroad, she never would have caught pneumonia and. . .and. . ." Real tears, not waterworks put on for Helen's benefit, escaped her eyes.

"I am so sorry." Helen's voice took on a tone of genuine compassion as she leaned over and tapped Dorothea's knee. "I know that one never really recovers from the death of one's parents. That is why I am glad you decided to spend a few weeks here in the country with us. The time away from the city will do you good."

"Yes."

"I want you to know that you can stay here with us as long as your heart desires. Never worry. Luke and I will not put you out."

"Thank you." Dorothea had no intention of asking to take up permanent or even semipermanent residence with her cousin, but the offer did her good.

"From the looks of the few bags you brought, you certainly could not survive here more than a fortnight or a month at best. The time will fly by all too rapidly."

She doesn't realize this is everything I have in the world now.

There was nothing more—either emotionally or physically—awaiting her in London. Her plan had been to take some of the money and find a respectable position as a nanny or governess. Room and board would of course be included in any such situation. Dorothea was determined to earn her own way. Never did she want to fall into the trap of being considered no more than a poor relation, passed off from distant relative to distant relative to rely on their Christian charity, possibly for the rest of her life. Such a situation was one she just couldn't endure. Never.

She only hoped to remain with Helen long enough to receive word from one of the inquiries she had already put out before she left. She supposed she should have rented a respectable room before she left, to provide a London address where responses could be sent, but she didn't want to spend an extra penny. And perhaps she could find a position in the country where she could remain near Helen, the closest family member she knew at the moment.

Dorothea opened her mouth to explain all to Helen, but Helen rose. "Well, now that is all settled, and you can enjoy yourself."

"But—"

"But nothing." She smiled. "Now make haste to don your favorite gown." She looked Dorothea over from head to toe. "I suggest a fine blue or green would go best with your light hair. Blue to flatter the color of your eyes."

"Yes, I possess such." Her skilled seamstress had made sure to fashion flattering gowns for Dorothea that didn't adopt the most extreme flights of vogue's fancy. Though sewn before her father's death, they remained well enough within current fashion dictates to prove acceptable for such an occasion.

"Jenny will show you to your quarters. Do hurry."

"I will." Now that she had eyed Lord Brunswick, Dorothea was determined not to miss another moment of the happy gathering.

Helen touched her shoulder. "And never forget, you need not worry about a thing."

Dorothea's conscience got the better of her. She couldn't delay telling Helen. "Oh, but I do."

Helen withdrew her comforting hand. "Whatever do you mean?"

"I have a confession to make. I did not come here just for a visit, but more." Dorothea looked at Helen's puzzled expression, and then the empty chair. "Perhaps you should return to your chair."

Helen hesitated, then plopped into the seat. "Did some-one die?"

"No. Have we not had enough of death in our family as of late?"

"Yes, but that does not always stop Providence."

"No, it does not. I have come to believe that the good Lord does have a plan for us all. I do not profess to understand His ways at all times, but I walk by faith as well as I can."

"And yet you are worried."

"Yes. I—I need money." There. She had said it. No matter what the outcome of her proclamation, she had finally managed to relieve herself of the burden of expressing her need. The very act left her feeling lighter.

"Oh, is that all?"

Helen's near dismissal of her problem gave her more courage. "Yes."

"In that case, we will discuss the amount later, and I shall have Luke write you a bank draft. If I make sure Cook prepares his favorite mutton stew for tomorrow's dinner, I might be able to convince him to part with as much as five hundred pounds." Helen tapped her fan against her fingers and sent Dorothea a conspiratorial smile.

Dorothea swallowed. "That. . .that is very generous of you, Helen. And I would accept such a sum gladly." She looked down at the beautiful, multicolored Oriental rug that showed wear on a few patches. An heirloom, no doubt. "But I fear that amount would hardly make a dent in the debts Father left." She lifted her face to meet Helen's gaze, half fearing her cousin's reaction.

Helen stiffened, and her eyes took on a light that expressed puzzlement and worry. "I hate to be the one to tell you this, Dorothea, but even here in the country those in the know were aware of your father's penchant for gambling."

"If you knew, why did you not say anything?" Anger at the fact that Helen let her humiliate herself by explaining her plight rose to her chest. Yet because she was in no position to assume a posture of righteous indignation, Dorothea tempered her feelings.

"I did not want to embarrass you. I had no idea your visit here would involve such a request. My uncle had never shown such irresponsibility before, and I had no reason to believe he had run through his entire fortune so quickly. I understand gaming was not his pastime of choice until after the death of your dear mother."

"True on all counts." A surge of embarrassment at thinking ill of her cousin filled Dorothea. She found she couldn't look her cousin in the eye, so she focused on a pair of ivory-colored silk draperies that decorated a window.

"So, if I may ask, just how much debt did your father leave?"

Shame replaced Dorothea's mere embarrassment, but she knew she couldn't deny Helen an answer. She had every right to ask. Still, in honor of her father's memory, Dorothea couched the dilemma in the best possible terms. She met Helen's gaze. "I have settled all but ten thousand pounds."

Helen flinched. "Ten thousand pounds?" Her eyes grew round.

Surprise gripped Dorothea. Helen was rumored to be wealthy enough that such an amount should have seemed almost like pocket change to her. Perhaps rumors were not so reliable after all.

"That is not an unheard-of sum." Helen drew herself up in a way that made Dorothea suspect she had discerned her unspoken thoughts and wanted to maintain her pride. "I do have some money set aside from my own inheritance, but of course Luke is responsible for my financial affairs."

So she planned to hide behind Luke. Dorothea couldn't blame Helen. If the situation were reversed, how would she feel about dipping into her capital to help a distant relative?

Helen continued, "Luke is generous with me, but I cannot count on his generosity if a request jeopardizes the future of our own heirs."

"I understand. Of course your husband is obliged to look after your interests. And I would never dream of creating hardship for you or my little niece." She made another attempt. "Although you do understand, I would pay you back, with interest."

"Oh. Indeed." Helen's voice shook ever so slightly. "But such an amount—that might take awhile to pay back?"

Dorothea lifted her chin. "I plan to take a job as a nanny or governess. Yes, I will need some time to pay it back because of course my wages will not be substantial. But I can also take in sewing and find other ways to earn extra money. And if you will have patience with me, you will find your good deed rewarded."

"Oh, but we could never allow you to take on employment!"

"Please, Helen, allow me to do what I must. I am determined not to be a burden to my family. If Luke will only agree—"

here to prove a point. That I do indeed possess a copy of *Letters from a Pennsylvania Farmer.*" Luke went to the shelf, retrieved an ancient leather volume, and held it up for his friend to see. "There, Lunenburg. I told you so."

"In that case, it is a good thing for me that you are not a gambling man. I would have lost quite a bit of money tonight. Instead, I found two lovelies. . . ." He looked Dorothea over from head to toe. "Discussing matters as grave and dull as finances."

Luke noticed Dorothea. "I beg your pardon. I was so intent on my project that I forgot my manners entirely."

"But you did address your wife. Not that I blame you. Her loveliness is not to be ignored," Baron von Lunenburg observed.

Helen giggled. "You are quite the flatterer."

"A flatterer? No, milady. I speak the truth. You are a woman who is easily noticed." Baron von Lunenburg then set his attentions upon Dorothea. He studied her in a way that made her feel like a diamond he was thinking of purchasing. She wasn't sure whether she should feel flattered or uncomfortable.

"I do not believe we have met?" he asked.

Dorothea said a silent prayer of thanks that her cousin possessed the good breeding and manners to make flawless introductions. She couldn't have spoken. Judging from the heat rising to her cheeks, Dorothea knew she must look like a boiled beet. Approaching Helen for a large sum of money to replace what her father had gambled away had been enough to embarrass her for the rest of her life, but now the guest of honor at the party—a stranger—had been privy to their conversation, as well? Judging from his inquisitive eyes and the way he licked his lips, she was beginning to reach the conclusion that Baron von Lunenburg was a lecherous stranger, at that.

"I am pleased to meet you, Baron von Lunenburg." Dorothea extended her hand out of habit rather than desire.

He kissed the back of her knuckles rather than brushing his lips against them in a gentle matter as she expected. She managed to keep from wincing.

Baron von Lunenburg peered into her face. "The pleasure is mine, I assure you. You have been hiding here in the study far too long. Surely you plan to join us. I do believe I have the right to insist, as a matter of fact, since the festivities have been presented in honor of my birthday."

"Of course," Helen interjected. "My cousin would never dream of doing anything less than what would please you, Baron von Lunenburg."

"And I would not dream of including myself in the celebration before changing out of this traveling suit and into a gown suitable for such an occasion," Dorothea said. "But as has been pointed out with such tact and eloquence, I have kept our hostess from the festivities too long. Please, Helen, return to your guests."

"In due time," Baron von Lunenburg said in a turnabout Dorothea hadn't expected. "First, I would like to address the matter about which I overheard you speaking. Am I to understand you are in need of two thousand pounds?"

The last thing Dorothea wanted was for another stranger to learn about her dire straits. She could only take the offensive. "You admit to me that you were eavesdropping on a private conversation? And you call yourself a gentleman?" Dorothea felt her face flush.

"Dorothea!" Helen admonished.

"I am sorry but—"

"Apologize this instant," Helen demanded.

"There is no need for all that." Baron von Lunenburg waved his hand to show how little importance he placed on Helen's suggestion. "The lady has a point. But I assure you that once you hear what I have to say you will be glad I overheard— quite by accident, I may add—about your dilemma. Now, how much do you owe? Two thousand pounds?"

Dorothea didn't know how to answer. That amount sounded

almost minuscule in comparison to what she really owed. "Uh—"

"I thought so. I would like to make you an offer."

"An offer? But I cannot think of—"

"There, there. Do not feel the need to be embarrassed," Baron von Lunenburg assured her. "We are all dear friends here. And even the finest lady can find herself a victim of circumstances beyond her control. That is the case with you, is it not?"

She nodded. "Yes."

"So you now find yourself in dire need of money?"

Dorothea felt her countenance turn to a feverish red, but her own false pride couldn't help her pay her debts. "Regrettably, yes. And the situation is far worse than you think. I am actually in need of not two thousand pounds, but ten thousand."

To her surprise, he didn't seem taken aback by the large sum. "That is a dilemma, but it does not have to be a ruinous one."

"Then you do not know the full extent of my circumstance. If I do not pay soon, I am threatened with the very real prospect of debtor's prison. Newgate, to be exact."

"Newgate. A wretched place. Not good enough to house even a common rodent." He shuddered with a violence that renewed Dorothea's fear of confinement in such a place. "Never mind a beautiful lady such as yourself."

Feeling a sudden chill, Dorothea rubbed her palms against her forearms.

"She will never enter Newgate as a convict," Helen assured him.

"So you are willing to settle her debts?"

"I—I have yet to confer with Luke."

Dorothea regarded Luke's demeanor and found little in the way of compassion in his expression.

Apparently noting the effect of the conversation on Dorothea, Baron von Lunenburg set his expression into a serious but kind facade. "Perhaps that will not be necessary. Tell me, just who are these creditors of yours? Merchants and bankers, I assume? Such types are known to be reasonable businessmen. Certainly they would be willing to work with you to keep you from such horror."

"If only my creditors were as you describe." Dorothea swallowed and cast her gaze at the floor. "But the people to whom I am indebted are proprietors of several gaming halls. I paid the honest merchants first—the ones I owed for coal, fabric, food, and any other legitimate services rendered."

"And you put off the gaming hall proprietors until last?"

She bored her gaze right into Baron von Lunenburg's eyes as she felt anger rise in her chest. "Yes. They took advantage of my father when he was in the throes of grief over my mother's death. Grief he never conquered. They knew he was wealthy and lent him money to gamble. Honest men would have stopped, but not these vile creatures. They did not care if he lost everything. And he did. Even after he had run through our entire fortune, he kept gambling, and they kept lending him money. Judging from my current situation, the pit is so deep I shall never get out as long as I live." She bowed her head and blinked back tears.

"So you think. But clearly you are an innocent sheep and not well acquainted with how to deal with insalubrious types. I, fortunately for you, am a man of the world."

His hopeful words encouraged her to look into his face. "Fortunately for me?"

"Yes. In fact, when I first heard about your plight, I had planned to offer you the money, but instead, I see that to solve your dilemma, I need only to call in a favor with a judge. Since your creditors operate just this side of the law, one well-placed word from him will assure that you never hear from them again. And you will be free from the prospect of Newgate—or any other prison—forever."

"Really?" The possibility seemed too fantastic to contemplate. "You can do that?"

He puffed out his chest. "Of course, my dear. I am Baron von Lunenburg."

"And you do not mind?"

"Mind? Why, of course not."

"But you owe me no favor. And the expense—"

His hand waved in a flippant manner that expressed his lack of concern. "The favor will cost me nothing."

"This is too wonderful for words! A gift from Providence, really." Helen rushed to Dorothea and drew her face close to hers. Dorothea caught a whiff of the tea rose scent Helen wore as her cousin whispered urgently, "I implore you not to be a fool, Dorothea. Do accept his offer!"

Dorothea pondered the suggestion. As she had many times, she mulled over in her mind a list of the people she could approach with reasonable expectation that they might be willing to offer her a hand up out of her quandary. The list came up too short to mention, especially now that Helen had offered such limited assistance.

She watched Baron von Lunenburg's expression as he studied her in return. A face not unpleasant to contemplate, she saw in it no traces of deceit. Yet his profession that the favor would cost him nothing didn't ring true. Surely he must have to pay something—if not money, then emotional bondage. What was his price for her?

"What are you waiting for, Dorothea?" Helen interjected into her musings. "If you do not respond soon and with a show of gratitude, Baron von Lunenburg is liable to withdraw his generous offer posthaste!"

"Even though I have not been apprised of the entire equation," Luke added, "I agree that, considering the direness of your current situation, to turn away such a munificent offer would seem as madness to me."

Dorothea stalled. "I have no argument with the fact that your offer is most generous, Baron von Lunenburg. And I assure you, I am quite grateful to you. But I must ask, begging your utmost pardon, if. . .if there is any way a person could question the propriety of asking a judge to intervene in such a matter?"

"Dorothea!" Helen's mouth dropped open.

"I beg your pardon, Helen, but your own reputation is just as much at stake as my own should this not be completely above board."

"True," Baron von Lunenburg agreed. "Which is why I would never think of putting my friends in jeopardy. What kind of man are you suggesting that I am, Lady Witherspoon?"

"A man I have only had the pleasure of meeting this evening, sir."

"Properly introduced to you by a party known to yourself," Baron von Lunenburg pointed out. His mustache frowned along with his mouth.

"How dare you question his honesty!" Helen cried. "Luke will soon be making a profitable investment with Baron von Lunenburg. Surely this is an indication that he is trustworthy. If you think it is not, then you are calling my husband a fool. And if you believe him to be a fool, then you should leave our house immediately!"

Spurred by the notion that she wished not to abandon herself to frigid, icy rain in the darkness outside, Dorothea mustered as much sincerity as she could. "I beg your pardon, Baron von Lunenburg."

"And?" Helen prompted.

Dorothea wasn't sure what Helen wanted her to say. "And?"

"Accept the offer."

Accept the offer? But what if Helen is wrong and it is dishonest? And even worse, what will Baron von Lunenburg expect in return?

She grasped at a last straw. "I assume that no favor will be expected of either Helen or Luke in return for helping me?"

"Indeed not!" Baron von Lunenburg sniffed.

"If I had anything to fear, I would not ask you to take the favor." Despite Helen's bravado, she glanced to Luke in an obvious side ploy to secure his approval.

"Indeed," Luke agreed. "I would trust Baron von Lunenburg with my life."

"Very well. I shall accept with untold gratitude the favor you offer me." Dorothea sent the baron a forced smile.

Baron von Lunenburg's mouth puckered in a way that almost seemed like a plea for a kiss. "The pleasure, I assure you, is my own."

❧

Lord Stratford Brunswick leaned against the wall even though his mother, God rest her soul, had taught him better. The party had proven to be a crashing bore, as events of this sort were liable to be.

He regarded the banquet table laden with all sorts of tempting pastries and appetizers but spied nothing new. Even nuggets of stuffed quail didn't seem different enough to spur him to try them. Since he had let his cook have the night off, Stratford wouldn't have another chance to eat an evening meal, so he contented himself with a piece of pork pie and a cherry tart.

Raking his gaze over the offerings, he noted that the same sumptuous treats appeared at all the parties, with little variation proving impossible simply because there was always so much food. Each hostess tried to serve more and better treats than the rest. From what he could see, the sheer number and variety of foodstuffs served by Helen had eclipsed the Crumpton gathering held the past week. Food at any party provided plenty of talk for the local gentry for weeks, sometimes even longer, but to Stratford's mind, such competition was vain in both senses of the word.

As he halfway listened to Halifax tell him yet again about his latest hunting expedition, he looked about the crowd and noted that the guest roster varied little from last week. That, he didn't mind. He took comfort in being around the same people, friends he had known for years. If being in their presence often meant listening to the same stories more than once, so be it.

He never lacked for people with whom to converse at any given function. As an eligible bachelor, Stratford's presence was expected. And of course, his marital status—or lack thereof—brought the matrons and their daughters running to him. Only one, an attractive but catty woman he had spurned as politely as he could last season, confined her conversation with him to greetings and salutations.

Few of the worldly crowd into which he was born and bred understood his level of faith, his true desire to walk as closely to the Lord as he could. Most of them preferred to visit God's house on Sundays, as was expected, and all but ignore Him except in the most perfunctory manner the rest of the week. Stratford knew he was a misfit of sorts; the type of woman he sought usually settled down with a vicar. Women in his set expected him to be more like the other worldly-wise and titled gentlemen they knew, and they had been reared to act according to those expectations.

Yet tonight he had seen someone who brought renewed interest to his heart. He had spotted a young woman hovering in the drawing room doorway. What was her business there? If only someone had been good enough to introduce them. He had looked around for her all night but never saw her beyond that initial eye contact from across the empty room. Had she been a beautiful vision, a dream beyond reality?

How silly. Of course he wasn't seeing visions. And no doubt once he became acquainted with her, she would prove to be just as frivolous as the rest.

Still, curiosity wouldn't let go of his thoughts.

He wondered why a woman would arrive in the midst of festivities unless as a guest. Maybe she lived far away, had somehow timed her arrival poorly, and was hoping to gain a position as a servant. No. The woman he had seen had been wearing a traveling suit that would have blended in with any worn by the other aristocratic ladies he knew. He doubted even the most prestigious servant could have afforded such a garment.

Could she be a nanny, perhaps? Sometimes ladies who had fallen on hard times resorted to such employment. A possibility, except he had overheard Helen telling the other women that she had the most superb nanny in the parish in her employ. So surely she wasn't looking for a new nanny.

Then who was the beautiful woman he had seen in the foyer?

He spotted Lunenburg, a fairly recent arrival to their parish, approaching. How could he avoid listening to the great Baron von Lunenburg boast, something he was sure to do if allowed to come within earshot. But approach him he did, and there was no way he could duck Lunenburg without appearing unforgivably rude.

"Brunswick, old boy! What a night this has been." Lunenburg took a swig of his drink with the vigor of a pirate who had just discovered a hidden cache of rum on the ship.

Stratford braced himself for a barrage of boasts. He didn't want to take the conversational bait, but courtesy demanded a response. Unable to think of anything witty that would distract Lunenburg from his intended topic, Stratford responded, "What a night, indeed."

Stratford noted Lunenburg's victorious smirk, and he held back a sigh.

Lunenburg leaned toward Stratford as though he were about to share a secret that, if overheard, would compromise the security of the empire. "I have pulled off quite a *coup*. Without any effort whatsoever—well, perhaps with a bit of effort." He curled his fingers and polished his nails against his frilled shirt, then inspected them with a look more suited to considering the acquisition of fine jewels than to checking the state of his fingernails.

Since his arrival in the parish, Lunenburg had made quite a show of boasting about how wise he was with money. He advertised himself as a businessman with concerns in a number of African mines and interests in America, as well. He spoke about his enterprises as though they were guaranteed investments sure to garner huge chests of money for their financiers.

Stratford wasn't so sure. In his ongoing efforts to be the best possible steward of his family fortune, he shied away from such risks. Yet he had witnessed Lunenburg in the act of convincing many a smart man that he should be part of such schemes. So far, Stratford didn't know of anyone who had invested with Lunenburg, but he suspected some people outside of their inner circle had taken the bait. What Stratford did know was that Lunenburg was in the process of procuring more investment partners for his concerns. His lure: that a new mine was being tapped, and slots for new backers might soon become available.

Intrigued, Stratford had listened to Lunenburg. He had every sales tactic down to a science—sense of urgency, rare opportunity, privileged inner-circle status. Stratford didn't doubt that Lunenburg would find willing—even eager— investors. But so far, he had not become one of them. Lunenburg had made it plain that he wanted to change Stratford's mind. He worked constantly, through efforts at friendship and nebulous references to the promise of more wealth, to spin Stratford into his web.

Knowing all this about Lunenburg, Stratford had no doubt that the man was about to brag that he had increased his number of shareholders or some other equivalent to the pot of money at the end of a rainbow.

"Do not keep me in suspense any longer," Stratford managed with as great a degree of interest as he could. "What did you accomplish with little or no effort?"

"The thing that every man wants to do from time to time, and especially when he is in a new place." He took another swig of his drink and announced, "I have secured for myself a lovely new mistress."

three

Stratford didn't answer right away.

"Are you envious, Brunswick?" Lunenburg asked. A slimy smirk curved his mouth. "I would be if I were you."

Stratford tightened his own lips in response. He wasn't surprised by Lunenburg's news. Since he had breezed into their parish two months ago, the baron had made it his business to worm his way into Stratford's social circle and to cut a fine figure at every event. In short time, he had become the center of everyone's attention, so much so that his friends were celebrating his birthday in a style more suited to a longtime friend than to a new acquaintance.

In a way, he could understand why. Men and women alike were captivated by Lunenburg's flattering words. Stratford enjoyed a compliment as much as the next man, but he had no intention of falling into a trap laid by his own vanity. He had a feeling that if he did, he would pay a dear price.

Stratford suspected Lunenburg to be a man who lusted more for money than women and decided to couch his response in way that would reflect that suspicion. "And I suppose your procurement of a new mistress—and your bold announcement of the fact—is intended to impress me with your investing prowess, as well?"

"I need not impress you when I have plenty of others eager to entrust me with their investments. And I must admit, I enjoy my little game of keeping you in great suspense by not telling you right away who the lucky lady is."

"Never let it be said you were one for modesty," Stratford quipped.

"A man of my talents has no need to put on a show of false humility." He inhaled deeply, as a victor surveying the spoils of war. "I am sure you are having trouble guessing which one is now my mistress since so many of the women in this room have made it known they have looked my way with interest." At that moment, he looked with interest at one woman in particular, a known flirt named Miss Morrow.

"I assume you mean she is the one." Stratford knew he shouldn't ask, but he couldn't help himself.

"Her?" He shook his head. "I would not stoop so low."

"Is that so? Most men think she is one of the prettiest in the parish."

"I am not most men. I concede that she is attractive, but she does not employ the type of discretion suitable to a man of my station. And of course, I do not want to compromise myself so that I am forced to take a wife before I am ready." He studied Stratford. "What about you? Are you among those men who consider Miss Morrow so comely?"

He shrugged. "Yes, but my taste runs in other directions." Stratford remembered the stunning, light-haired beauty standing in the shadows. He set his glance over the crowd of women wearing dresses in an array of colors and men in their best evening suits but saw only familiar faces. Where was the blond?

He had about given up hope he would see her again that evening.

"The blond, perhaps?"

"The blond." Stratford startled as a pang of unwarranted jealousy ripped through his stomach. "I beg your pardon?" ·

"The one in the corner, waving her fan in our direction."

He eyed the woman in question, and a sense of relief washed over him. "Oh. That blond. Fan waving or not, she is on the brink of betrothal to Lord Evanston."

"Ah. Then I would deduce that she is on the brink of conquest, too. Surely she would enjoy one last flirtation before confining herself to the dull duties of a matron."

Stratford knew Evanston to be hot-tempered. "I would not prod that hornet's nest with a stick if I were you."

"No matter. My new mistress is entering at this moment." Lunenburg looked eastward.

Stratford followed Lunenburg's glance to an arched entryway on the far side of the room. The woman was wearing a blue gown, and her light hair was curled into ringlets on either side of her face, a style that had become popular in recent years. Most of her hair was covered by a broad ribbon in the same color that had some sort of proper name, one he couldn't remember.

But when she turned her face toward the fire, he saw those blue eyes and lips as pink as a spring rose. Stratford nearly dropped his glass of lemonade. "Her? That is the one?"

"Indeed." Lunenburg smiled, then took another swig of his drink.

Jealousy returned with a vengeance. Stratford tried to put on an appearance of maintaining his composure by drawing himself up to his full height and taking in a breath. "She is new here, is she not?"

"You should be more privy to that knowledge than I, since you have been a lifelong resident here." The baron smiled with the expression of one who held the key to secret knowledge. "I know. I am a sore winner. I should not tease you in such a manner. Of course you do not know her. That, my friend, is Lady Dorothea Witherspoon, Helen's cousin visiting from London."

Lady Dorothea Witherspoon from London. So that was the identity of his mystery woman.

"Lovely, is she not?" Lunenburg prompted.

Too lovely for you.

The image of Lunenburg embracing the woman that Stratford had admired from afar left his stomach roiling. He swallowed. "Uh, yes. She is lovely. Quite so. And I hardly think a lady with a title would agree to be your mistress—or anyone else's."

"Now, now, old man. She has not agreed yet. But titled or not, once she has heard my sweet words whispered in her ear in the dark, no doubt she will."

"You seem a bit too confident."

"I admit that I have more than sweet words to offer." Lunenburg's empty smile didn't reach his eyes. "No, let us say—my timing was such that I was able to step in and do her a monumental favor, which placed me in the happy position of becoming the recipient of her gratitude."

"Gratitude is a thin thread on which to base a romantic alliance."

"If you think such, then you underestimate the power of gratitude."

Stratford studied Dorothea. She seemed oblivious to any arrangement. He noticed that she didn't once make an effort to catch Lunenburg's attention or even send him wily but knowing glances. Her face radiated innocence, not the sly look of a woman of the world. He had an odd feeling. "Then I suppose you are not worried that anyone else will flatter her with beautiful words and lure her away from you."

"Worried, no." Though they had been speaking in a volume too low to be overheard, Lunenburg brought his voice down to a near whisper. "But of course I must not be too obvious about our relationship, which is why I have made no effort to be by her side in this crowd tonight. I would not want to embarrass a lady of fine breeding and well-placed station."

"Then you will not mind in the least if I greet her." Not waiting for a response, Stratford strolled toward Dorothea.

❧

Dorothea tried not to break off her conversation in midsentence. She looked in the center of the crowd and noticed people parting like the Red Sea to let the man she wanted to meet pass. He was strolling toward her with such speed he looked as though someone were chasing him. She hadn't expected him to look even more handsome in the more intense lighting of the hall. Her brief memory was of the man standing in the shadows. His countenance and form, she noted happily, were no disappointment.

Dorothea fiddled with the fan she held and swallowed to ease her throat, which had become dry with nervous anticipation. She had been told she was attractive but didn't dare flatter herself with the notion that she appeared so enchanting that men were running to meet her. Yet he did seem to be in a hurry.

"I might have known," Helen muttered.

"Known what?"

"Never mind," Helen whispered. She turned her voice up several notches as the man reached them. "There you are, Stratford. I was wondering how long it would take you to notice my cousin."

"So you think I make a study of all the women, do you, Helen? Am I such a rogue as all that?"

His melodious voice, its tone hinting at adventure and excitement, made Dorothea's knees threaten to buckle. Was he a rogue? Rogue enough to lift her into his arms and take her away on his fine stallion, away from all memories of the evening's degradation? If only he were a rogue, indeed!

She waved her fan over her cheeks too rapidly to be considered polite.

Helen shot her a warning look and responded to Stratford's jest. "I do not suppose you are too much the cad for me to offer you a proper introduction to my distant cousin." As promised, she complied.

Lord Stratford Brunswick. So Helen was right—this is the man I described! And a fine man he seems to be, indeed.

"I am enchanted by your presence, Lady Witherspoon."

Lord Brunswick took her hand in his and brushed his lips against the back of her knuckles. The soft motion left her wobbling with such joy that she found herself searching for an empty chair. Since the few seats available were occupied by dowagers and elderly men, she saw that she would have to stand on her own two feet. She hoped they would hold her up as she steadied knees that quaked anew.

She resumed wild fanning even though they were

positioned nowhere near the crackling fire. Now that she had gathered enough courage to look at him for more than an instant, she realized he was just as handsome up close as he had been from a distance. And the way his gaze held hers, she sensed she had piqued his interest, as well.

"Dorothea," Helen prodded, "you have not yet been introduced to Lady Wickford."

"Before you leave my presence, might I inquire how long we here in our little parish might enjoy the pleasure of your presence, Lady Witherspoon?" Lord Brunswick asked.

Dorothea ignored her cousin's hand tugging on her arm. She kept her focus right on his face, a face of fine contours framed by hair as black as coal. "My cousin has graciously extended me an invitation to remain here for a fortnight."

"Only a fortnight? But I should hope for longer. Perhaps she could be convinced to allow you an extended stay." Sparkling eyes the blue color of lapis lazuli stones mesmerized her. She leaned her face as closely to his as she dared without being too forward.

"I may not need convincing." A strangely husky voice left her lips. Did such an intonation really belong to her?

"Indeed." Helen's voice sounded sharp.

Dorothea cut her glance her cousin's way and discovered that Helen glowered. She chose to ignore her cousin. Whatever foul mood of Helen's she might endure could be tolerated for a fortnight in exchange for a few moments of idle conversation with Lord Brunswick. Especially since he seemed ever so amenable.

A matron who had been introduced to Dorothea earlier as Lady Rose Morgan tapped Helen on the shoulder and flew into a glowing recitation of the delights of the food that Helen had served. Judging from the way Helen didn't look Lady Morgan straight in the eye, Dorothea could tell she regretted the interruption. Dorothea felt thankful that Lady Morgan insisted Helen accompany her to the table to discuss the merits of an astounding array of fruit tarts. With a sniff and another admonishing look sent Dorothea's way, Helen left her side. Finally. Now she could listen to whatever this fascinating man had to say without reprisal.

Dorothea considered his suggestion that she remain longer than a fortnight. She had already been introduced to a number of people who seemed pleasant enough, but of course anyone can seem pleasant during a brief introduction from a mutual friend.

Her present surroundings offered reason to stay. Once she had warmed herself by the inviting fire, Dorothea felt at home, for Helen's taste in decor mirrored her mother's. Deep blue draperies fashioned from heavy velvet insulated the room from any draft that could enter through the windows and stood out before cream and gold damask wallpaper. The floor was barely visible in such a crowded room, but what spots emerged now and again looked to be polished. Maple wood planks shone in the candlelight.

For the first time that day, she was glad she'd been sitting in a cramped coach all afternoon. Her feet weren't tired, so now that she had recovered somewhat from the initial impact of meeting Lord Brunswick, she was able to resist the temptation to steal a chair from an aging dowager.

Let them have their chairs, she thought. Their years of standing all night at a crowded gathering had passed them by long ago. All too soon, she would become a dowager. In mourning and preoccupied with the cares of debt for so long, Dorothea had felt and acted like someone thirty years her senior. Finally, the time to be young again had arrived. The notice had been brought to her attention and punctuated by Lord Stratford Brunswick.

"If only I could remain here not a fortnight, but forever," Dorothea ventured.

He surveyed his surroundings. "Fallen in love with the place already?"

With the place?

"An easy task, to be sure," she said aloud.

"To be sure." He took a swallow out of the glass of lemonade he was holding. She noticed that he didn't do so until he eyed a similar glass in her hand. "How good that you are able to visit your cousin. You certainly chose an auspicious time, since practically everyone in the parish is in attendance tonight."

"Yes, the number of introductions has been a bit overwhelming, but I am sure I will be able to remember everyone important. I will certainly have no trouble recalling your face and name." She felt yet another blush. She couldn't remember a time when she had said something so bold to a man—a man barely known to her, at that. Her fan set itself into motion again.

"And I, yours."

Feeling the need to redeem herself, Dorothea searched for a way to reveal the paramount role that faith played in her life. "Since I have spent all day in my journey from London, I am grateful that I will have tomorrow to rest before being expected to rise for church on Sunday. I trust you attend the lovely white church in the village?"

"Yes, I do. As does everyone else, whether truly devout or not."

"Only the truly devout would make such an observation. You must be a man of meditation and prayer yourself."

"I devote time to the Lord outside of attending church, yes. Although I never feel I am Christian enough or that I can ever spend too much time with Him."

"You hunger for Him, then." She prayed the answer would be in the affirmative. If so, then truly Lord Brunswick was a man after her own heart.

He became pensive. "I have never heard the sentiment expressed in such a way, but I do believe that could describe me." He looked into her eyes. "I hope you do not find my devotion to the Savior off-putting."

"No, indeed. Not in the least." She wanted to elaborate, but she had already been far too forthright in her speech that evening.

Baron von Lunenburg chose that moment to approach them. "Well, Brunswick, I see you are attempting to monopolize the most beautiful woman in this room tonight." He turned his gaze to Dorothea. "He always does that, you know."

"Oh, he does?" Dorothea's chest tightened with a jealousy she had no right to feel toward unnamed women.

"Baron von Lunenburg exaggerates," Lord Brunswick assured her. "I assume the two of you have met?"

"Yes, we have." Dorothea debated whether she should reveal any of her business to Stratford. For reasons unknown to her, she felt led to share some of the details, though doing so went against her natural reticence. But when she followed her instincts, she usually found a reward. "I have already discovered Baron von Lunenburg to be a most generous man. He offered to do me a great favor, which has eased my mind considerably."

"Oh, how generous of him. And he asks for nothing in return?" Lord Brunswick eyed Baron von Lunenburg.

Baron von Lunenburg didn't give Dorothea a chance to respond. "My, Brunswick, but you seem concerned with the affairs of others." He looked at Dorothea. "You will find in a small parish out here in the country, there is little to distract people from idle gossip and the act of being busybodies."

"I beg your pardon," Lord Brunswick countered.

Dorothea answered, "That is quite all right. I am the one who broached the subject. Lord Brunswick was merely being polite."

"Never let it be said that I argued with a lady," Baron von Lunenburg responded.

"If you will excuse me." Lord Brunswick nodded.

Dorothea tried not to allow her gaze to linger upon his retreating frame. Of course he had to speak to other guests, and etiquette demanded that she not allow one man to dominate her time, as well. Too bad.

"Shall we see the gardens?" Baron von Lunenburg took her elbow in a possessive manner she wasn't sure she liked.

And she had some idea that flowers weren't all he wanted to admire.

She shuddered so he could see she felt chilly. "The night air does not always suit me."

"You are feeling a bit cold?"

"Yes, even in this room with all these people and a roaring fire." She studied the flames to keep from looking at the way his jaw had set into a hard line.

"I trust you are not always so icy."

She shuddered with a real chill this time and looked back at him. "Whatever do you mean?"

At that moment, Helen tapped her on the shoulder to introduce her to the vicar. Never was Dorothea so glad to see a man of the cloth.

four

Stratford chatted with a lady of considerable pedigree and lesser comeliness whose mother had led her to him, but his mind was far from idle conversation. He focused his eyes on Lunenburg from time to time, enough to track his movement throughout the room. He had to speak to the man before the celebration ended. A few less energetic partygoers had already departed. If he didn't make his move soon, he would miss his opportunity.

As soon as he could comfortably excuse himself, Stratford made his way through the crowd and back to Lunenburg.

"I need to speak with you."

"My, but you are talkative tonight." Lunenburg's voice held an edge he hadn't noticed before. Obviously his mood had fouled.

"I am only as talkative as is necessary. I have a matter of some urgency to discuss with you, one that could affect the future of us both. If you will permit me."

"This is a private matter?" A greedy light glimmered in Lunenburg's eyes. Stratford recognized the expression. Lunenburg thought he had just surrendered himself to be a part of one of his financial schemes. Well, let him think that, if that's what it took to garner the man's attention.

"Yes, it is a private matter."

"Then let us adjourn to the library."

Lunenburg led Stratford out of the room and into a chilly hallway with the ease of one familiar with the ins and outs of the estate house. How quickly he had made himself at home among them all. Stratford could only hope that the trust of his friends wasn't misplaced.

"We are in luck," Lunenburg noted upon entering the library.

Stratford noticed it was empty of people but stuffed with shelves of books that covered all four walls and extended by two rows into the center of the room, as well. The smell of aging leather book covers and fine paper defined the room.

"We can have complete privacy." Lunenburg took a seat in a large chair upholstered in brown leather and leaned toward Stratford as he took the nearest seat. "So, what urgent matter took me away from all the pretty ladies at the party?"

"A pretty lady, in fact. The one you say is now your mistress."

He leaned back so his back touched the chair. "Oh. Her."

Stratford couldn't contain his surprise. "I must say, the blush of new love seems to have worn off quickly. Rebuffed already?"

Lunenburg cleared his throat. "Of course not."

"If you have not been, I venture that you soon will be."

"By my own mistress? What a ridiculous notion."

"Not so ridiculous if your presumed mistress does not realize what is expected of her. And I have a feeling, based on a brief conversation I just shared with Lady Witherspoon, that she has not an inkling of the unspoken aspect of your arrangement."

"Really? Surely you jest."

"I do not remember a time when I have been more serious."

Lunenburg didn't answer right away. "I must admit, she played the innocent babe when we spoke, but I thought she was putting on a show for the benefit of her relatives. But in actuality, I find it hard to believe she thinks I am doing her a great favor for free. Certainly she cannot be so naive."

"What makes you think she is not naive?"

"From all appearances, she is past the age of consent, and I have been told that she was born and reared in London."

"I am aware that in our ribald day and age a creature of such virtuousness is rare, but I do believe we have found an orchid among daisies." He didn't wait for Lunenburg to comment. "And because Lady Dorothea is a sheltered orchid, I would implore you not to follow through with granting whatever favor you were seeking for her."

"You have no idea what you are asking."

"Do I not? What trouble is she in, then?"

"Costly trouble. She is in debt in the amount of ten thousand pounds."

With the greatest of effort, Stratford hid his shock. "That much, eh?" He made quick calculations of his bank balances in his head and deciphered favorable numbers. "Whom does she owe?"

"An assortment of creditors in London. Some of them are not so savory types."

He couldn't imagine how Dorothea could have associated with anyone from the underworld or have encountered ways to spend such a large amount of money. "How—"

"Her father gambled away her fortune. The proprietors of the gaming halls are demanding payment."

"Indeed? What a shame. I cannot imagine any responsible man losing a fortune at such an unworthy enterprise."

"Perhaps you cannot, but many a man, of high rank or servant, has given in to the temptation to gamble." Lunenburg rubbed his forefinger and thumb together as if fingering an imaginary coin.

Stratford searched his mind for a solution. "Surely she has valuables she can sell."

Lunenburg crossed one leg over the other. "She has already sold everything, including her home and family jewelry."

"Yet she is still in debt by such a large amount." Stratford let out a low whistle when he considered how deeply Lord Witherspoon must have gotten himself into financial straits. "I assume you agreed to step in and pay the difference."

"In a way. I promised to ask a judge I know to speak to her creditors so they would forgive the remainder of her debts."

"You have that kind of influence?" Stratford tried not to show how the fact impressed him.

"When your name is Baron Hans von Lunenburg, your influence can be felt quite widely." His chest puffed out ever so slightly.

"So Baron Hans von Lunenburg is not above using strong-arm tactics to settle the matter."

Lunenburg shrugged. "Do you really feel sympathetic toward the unsavory types who run gaming establishments?"

Since the man brought up a valid point, Stratford considered his opinion. "No, I cannot say I sympathize with them in the least. I believe they prey on the weakest members of our society, whether the weak are rich men who are unable to resist temptation or the poor who dream of an easy path to riches. But I surmise the operators of gaming houses would argue that they provide a service, too. Entertainment and amusement for the bored and lonely. And since no one forces anyone to frequent a gaming establishment, they could also counter that if anyone finds trouble there, he has no one to blame but himself."

Lunenburg applauded, leaving a large pause between each clap, an obvious display of sarcasm.

Stratford remained silent, knowing that to take the bait would be folly.

"Bravo," Lunenburg concluded. "So what are you saying?"

"I am saying that although I am not fond of their type of business, robbing Lord Witherspoon's creditors does not seem to be the Christian thing to do."

Lunenburg chuckled, but his laugh held no mirth. "Are you as virtuous as you portray yourself?"

The backhanded compliment felt like a slap. "I do not offer women favors based on deceit or engage in heavy-handedness to defraud creditors."

"Ah, but I only asked one woman." His crooked smile indicated he fancied himself quite witty.

Stratford responded with a stony silence.

"Then you are a more virtuous man than I. And therefore I venture you enjoy far less than I do in the way of amusement."

"Once a man decides to follow the Lord to the best of his ability, illicit pleasures may offer some temptation but become much easier to resist."

"Then you must be a very lonely man." He pulled on the end of his mustache.

Stratford entwined his fingers. "I would rather be lonely than to wallow in sin. Of course, I pray that the Lord will send me a wife in His time."

"Enough with your religious talk. I feel as though I have entered a monastery."

"If you were to enter a monastery, would you know where you were?" Stratford couldn't help asking.

"I would probably know enough to run out of it as fast as I could." Lunenburg looked toward each table. "If only Luke kept a supply of cigars and brandy here. I could use a bracing drink and a good smoke."

"Allow me to suggest that if you spent less time drinking and smoking, you would find a virtuous wife."

"I am not in the market for such a commodity."

"Obviously."

Lunenburg sighed. "I had no idea Dorothea was such a fool. Perhaps she thought she was safe because Helen encouraged her to take the favor."

"I would not count Helen as a woman of the world, either. But surely Luke had some notion."

Lunenburg shrugged. "I would wager that Luke was more interested in maintaining his own fortune than in maintaining Dorothea's virtue."

"Which I have reason to believe remains intact. And unless you plan to make her an offer of courtship, I suggest you not sully her."

"Indeed? You sound more like a man in love than a disinterested stranger. Do you know Dorothea from some-where else?"

Stratford couldn't say he did. And from Lunenburg's vantage point, he must look like a fool for intervening in the affairs of a woman he had only met that night. But he had to. He just had to.

Stratford cleared his throat before he spoke. "Since you

obviously have no intention of honoring Lady Dorothea with a legitimate proposal of marriage, I suggest that you save your favor with the judge for a more profitable occasion and allow me to take care of her debt instead."

"What? Perhaps you are the one who needs a stiff drink."

"No. I am perfectly sober and do not regret what I just said."

"So you want to spend a fortune helping a woman you only met this evening? I truly do not understand the English code of honor." His eyebrows rose. An ugly laugh escaped from Lunenburg's lips, its sound echoing throughout the room. "I think I see. In spite of all your religious talk, you have a secret motive, you sly dog. You want her for yourself."

Stratford didn't answer. Perhaps he did want her for himself. He couldn't deny the sparks he felt flying when she was near. Looking into her face, with eyes so bright and skin so smooth, framed by perfect curls that could be compared to whirling cascades of yellow diamonds, he could imagine drinking in her beauty every day for the rest of his natural life.

He considered the likelihood that he was too taken by the loveliness of her face, the beauty of her form, and the lilt of her voice to make a reasoned and proper judgment. Perhaps Dorothea held no future for him. Possibly she was meant to step into his life for an instant to offer him a test of how he would respond to another Christian in trouble, only to return to London forever. And if so, he was determined to pass the test. He felt compelled to deliver this innocent young woman from her debt—and from Lunenburg's clutches.

"What do you care?" Stratford retorted with more vehemence than he meant to express. "You have as much as admitted that she is not promising as a mistress. Why not procure a lady with your charms? Consider my offer an act of kindness toward you. I am taking a bad deal off your hands. One you apparently entered into unwisely and in haste."

Lunenburg drummed the fingertips of both hands against each other. "I am not sure the transaction I made is as flawed as you proclaim. As you mentioned, my charms are considerable, and I may be able to change her mind. She would not be the first woman to fall in love with me after hearing my sweet words and feeling my warm embrace."

Stratford pictured Lunenburg's arms around Dorothea and flinched. He didn't dare speak his mind.

Please, Lord, let Lunenburg see reason.

Lunenburg let the moment of silence drag before answering. "Let me counter your proposal. What if you sweeten the deal with a hundred pounds for my trouble? If you do, then Lady Dorothea Witherspoon—and her load of debt—are all yours."

A hundred pounds. A reasonable price indeed. He didn't hesitate. "Done. I will send a bank draft by messenger to you first thing in the morning."

"Very well." Lunenburg looked both relieved and elated as he got up from his seat. Stratford followed suit. Lunenburg extended his hand, and Stratford shook it, sealing the agreement.

Stratford lifted his forefinger. "Oh, and one last thing."

Lunenburg stiffened. "Our contract is set. We shook hands."

"And I will live up to my part of the agreement. What I ask now will cost you nothing. I only request that no one is to be made aware of our arrangement."

Shock covered Lunenburg's expression. "No one? Not even the lady herself?"

"That is right."

Lunenburg crossed his arms. "But why?"

"Because I use scripture as my guide. The sixth chapter of the book of St. Matthew proclaims, 'But when thou doest alms, let not thy left hand know what thy right hand doeth: that thine alms may be in secret: and thy Father which seeth in secret himself shall reward thee openly.'"

"I said it before and I will say it again. Your rabid talk of religion does not fool me," Lunenburg responded. "I know what reward you seek, and your reward is not from a father."

Stratford's patience had expired. "How dare you. I have

had enough of your insults. In my grandfather's day, such talk would have led to a duel. A contest you, Baron von Lunenburg, would lose."

"Let us not resort to hysteria, old man." He strode toward the door leading to the hallway—and safety—but not before Stratford heard him mutter, "I shall never understand men who give such credence to their Bibles."

five

The following day, Dorothea took lunch with Luke and Helen. She still reeled from the events that had taken place in short succession the previous evening: seeing and becoming interested in Lord Brunswick, revealing to Helen the reason for her visit, and then being rescued from financial ruin and prison by Baron von Lunenburg, not to mention meeting many of her hosts' friends in the parish. All in all, the evening had turned into a success beyond her wildest expectations.

And here she sat, enjoying a meal of mutton, green peas, baby potatoes seasoned with parsley, and aromatic tea laced with cinnamon. The meal was served on pink floral-patterned bone china and a deeply etched silver service placed on sturdy but elegant embroidered muslin. Dorothea, Helen, and Luke dined surrounded by tasteful decor and subdued paintings of botanical arrangements.

Dorothea recalled her luncheon taken the previous day. The carriage, run by a business concern that catered to those who could ill afford the best accommodations, had stopped at a nondescript inn for the midday meal. There she had been served thin soup that the cook claimed to include chicken but didn't, dark bread too tough to throw to the dog, and a flavorless brown beverage that purported to be tea. The company wasn't any better. They ate among rough, unkempt men who enjoyed expressing their approval of brassy serving wenches with firm slaps on the rump that sent both parties into peals of laughter. Dorothea herself didn't escape the notice of one leering man in particular, a development that didn't help her relax during her meal.

How glad she was to be visiting refined relatives, however

distant their blood connection. The previous evening after the birthday celebration concluded, Dorothea had retired to the comfortable and well-appointed bedchamber Helen had assigned to her. Before she crawled into bed, Dorothea had gotten down on her knees to thank the Lord and sent praises to heaven for the blessing of being relieved from her insurmountable debt and for Helen's gracious hospitality. That night, Dorothea slumbered soundly for the first time in months, so long that she missed breakfast. Helen didn't even chastise her. With each passing moment, Dorothea's gratitude concerning her improved situation diminished not a whit.

The present day's company proved much more to Dorothea's liking, as well. Her excitement from a successful party still evident, Helen spent most of the luncheon hinting for Dorothea to compliment the food, atmosphere, and music provided by a string quartet. Dorothea complied, but concurrently she thought of the names and faces of those she had met the previous night.

"You know, Baron von Lunenburg is quite the eligible bachelor," Helen reminded her. "I have no doubt he has taken a special shine to you since he made such a grand gesture to see to it that your debts are forgiven."

Fear made an unwelcome call on Dorothea. "I hope he does not change his mind."

"Of course he will not," Luke assured her. "Lunenburg is a man of his word." He drank from his cup, then set it down with a firm motion. Dorothea watched steam float from the tea remaining. "So. When will Lunenburg be calling on you?"

The question took Dorothea by surprise. "Did he ask to call on me?"

Luke squirmed in his seat. "I assumed he would be calling on you very shortly after what transpired last night."

Though Baron von Lunenburg was attractive in his way, and though he no doubt had done her a favor she could never repay, Dorothea had no interest in him as a suitor.

Lord Brunswick had piqued her interest far too much. "Since you are the man of the house, I would be most grateful to you if you could discourage Baron von Lunenburg."

"What?"

"I am ever so sorry if I appear to be ungrateful. I assure you, I am not. I shall hold Baron von Lunenburg in the highest esteem for as long as I live, and if I can do any favor for him, I shall. But I simply am not interested in him romantically. Because of my feelings, I do not want to encourage him. I believe to do so would only be dishonest and a cruel disservice to us all."

Helen reached for Dorothea's hand and grabbed her by the fingers. "Do not be a ninny, Dorothea. Baron von Lunenburg has shown you great interest. You must reciprocate."

"But—"

"At the very least, give him a chance. I know you will find him quite charming and pleasant once you have spent time in relative privacy with him."

"I am sure," Luke muttered.

"What is that, my dear?" Helen let go of Dorothea's hand.

"Nothing." He cleared his throat, but the women kept staring at him. "Uh. . .it just seems now that I need to have a word with Lunenburg—after he has called in the favor, that is. I am afraid there has been a great misunderstanding on Dorothea's part. And on yours, as well, Helen."

"Whatever do you mean?"

"I think Lunenburg was expecting Dorothea to be quite attentive to him in return for the favor. Having no idea what type of woman Dorothea was, I assumed all parties understood the implicit meaning of the conversation and that the arrangement was agreeable to all."

Implicit meaning? What implicit meaning?

Dorothea leaned forward. "I confess I was never any good at playing games, so I have no idea what you mean, and I have a feeling I do not wish to learn."

"A good conjecture, considering that you are apparently a

fine Christian woman," Luke agreed.

"Thank you, although I have no idea why you would assume the opposite to be true. In any event," Dorothea continued, "I specifically asked if I would be required to do anything at all in return for Baron von Lunenburg's actions, and he said he expected nothing. You heard him." Dorothea sent a pleading look Helen's way. "And so did you."

"Yes," Helen confirmed.

"After his assurances," Dorothea said, "I assumed Baron von Lunenburg was acting out of Christian charity."

"Christian charity. Hmm," Luke said. "Yes, I can see that you have led a sheltered life. Not unlike my dear Helen."

"Sheltered or not, you still owe Baron von Lunenburg your utmost courtesy, for the sake of our family's reputation," Helen said. "You cannot come here and then treat our friends in any way that could be construed as less than gracious."

"I understand. I will be polite."

"See that you are," Helen warned her.

"Speaking of our friends," Luke said, "Brunswick has asked if he might pay us a call later this afternoon."

"Oh!" So Lord Brunswick wanted to see her again already? Dorothea tried not to lose control of her teacup.

"You must have made quite an impression on him, as well. You have been here only one evening, and already two men are chasing you as bees chase after pollen. Good for you." Helen cut into her mutton. "But really, I advise you to keep your attentions focused on Baron von Lunenburg. He is a much better match for you, I think."

"I noticed he is quite the popular figure," Dorothea observed.

"And for good reason," Luke observed. "He has made many people quite a lot of money."

"That is not a very good reason for popularity, in my opinion."

"There are worse." Helen took a sip of tea. "At least with the attention you have garnered, your fortnight here promises to be interesting."

Dorothea was glad she had a piece of fork-tender mutton

practically melting amid gravy in her mouth, which offered excuse enough for her not to respond. She didn't want to return to London. The room she had planned to rent was cheap and dreary. She wasn't sure if she would even like the other boarders.

Heavenly Father, release me from this false pride.

Soon the exhausting trip and eventful evening caught up with Dorothea despite the invigorating effects of the tea Helen served. She only wished to retire to her room for a short nap before Lord Brunswick was due to arrive for tea at four that afternoon. She didn't want him seeing her looking less than her best. She was about to offer excuses to her hosts when the butler entered, begged pardon for the interruption, and handed Luke a calling card.

He barely scanned the name before he looked at Dorothea. "Why, Baron von Lunenburg has come to call for Dorothea."

"You were not expecting him," Dorothea surmised. Indeed, she had not been expecting him, either. Not after she had refused to go with him to the garden.

Helen gasped. "No, indeed. Well, the men are apparently taking full advantage of your short time here. You just might gain two proposals of marriage before your visit is through." She all but clapped her hands in approval.

"I would not be so vain as to venture such a guess." Nevertheless, Dorothea felt a blush rise to her cheeks.

Moments later she greeted Baron von Lunenburg in the drawing room. As the afternoon waned past teatime, she realized why everyone found him captivating. She expected him to brag about his shrewd investments for others, but he focused his conversation on her beauty and their mutual interest in gardening. She speculated that he didn't bother to talk about money since the fact that she had none to invest was well known to him—and, independent or not, she was still a member of the fairer sex.

She listened as he spun fascinating tales of travel, both firsthand experiences and those told to him by interesting acquaintances. Hints that he had other entertaining yarns in store left her wanting to learn more about him. He insisted that she address him by his Christian name of Hans and had just shared the highlight of an amusing event that occurred in the Prince Regent's court—leaving her laughing—when Helen entered.

"I do hate to interrupt," Helen apologized with a smile on her face. "Obviously both of you are having such an enjoyable time together. I am so pleased. And I trust your tea and biscuits were satisfactory?"

Hans hurried to his feet in deference to Helen. "More than satisfactory. You always serve the most aromatic and exquisite blend of tea leaves. Please, you must reveal to me the source of your supply."

"But if I do," she quipped, "then you will have no reason to come by for tea."

"On the contrary, I will have every reason to come by— and not necessarily just for tea." He gave Dorothea a pleasing sidelong glance.

Dorothea knew that Helen's willingness to interrupt her visit with Hans signaled that something could be amiss, so she quickly turned serious. "Is everything all right?"

An odd look crossed her face and then vanished just as quickly. "Yes. Fine. Just fine. Uh, Dorothea, I must ask you to excuse yourself."

Dorothea was puzzled until she remembered what had to be the reason for Helen's interruption. Lord Brunswick! Had he come to call? If so, indeed she must go to him.

"Of course I shall excuse myself." She looked into Hans's face. "By your leave."

"Of course." He glanced at the mantel clock. "I have stayed long enough."

Indeed, two hours had passed, albeit quickly.

"Please do feel at liberty to visit us again in the near future," Helen said.

Hans donned the hat the butler handed him and allowed

him to assist with his overcoat. "I regret that I cannot spend even more time in Lady Dorothea's company today. But surely if I were to linger any longer, I would be accused of monopolizing her time unfairly." He turned his eyes toward her. "We will enjoy a repeat of today soon, I trust."

"Of course," Helen promised and stepped aside so he could exit.

The front door had just shut behind him when Helen took her by the wrist and hissed, "Lord Brunswick is waiting for you in the library."

"Oh, dear!" Dorothea tried to discern the best course of action. "Could you occupy him while I take a moment to freshen myself?"

Helen nodded. "Are you this popular in London?"

"A girl in mourning is hardly popular. Perhaps now that my time of formal mourning is past—and I am out here in the country—I am blossoming into a butterfly."

"A social butterfly," Helen pointed out. "Let me caution you once more. If I were you, I would concentrate my energies on the one departing. Keep your visit with the one in the library to a minimum."

And as soon as she saw Lord Brunswick waiting for her, Helen's words faded.

He rose to greet her. She extended her hand, and he complied with the most obligatory brush of his lips and, to her disappointment, hurried to release it.

"I beg your pardon for interrupting what was obviously a very amusing visit between you and Baron von Lunenburg."

His chilly greeting took her aback. She clutched at her throat. "An amusing visit?"

"I recognized the carriage in the drive as belonging to him."

"Oh."

"And your laughter could be heard in the hallway."

"You wouldn't ask me to put on a dour expression for a polite social caller, would you?"

"I suppose not." His concession seemed to be forced.

As Dorothea chose a brown leather seat across from Lord Brunswick and then smoothed her day frock the color of mellowed ivory, she noticed a fresh pot of tea and a plate of biscuits waiting on the table for the two of them. The pleasant though bitter fragrance of the hot beverage usually offered Dorothea the temptation to enjoy an interlude of refreshment, but not on this occasion. And another biscuit, even those emanating the tart scent of lemon and with a moist appearance that told her butter had been added generously, was the last morsel Dorothea wanted to eat since she had just indulged. But for the sake of manners, she took a small, round, buttery treat with a dollop of lemon curd in the center.

Burning logs crackled in the fireplace. Though they relied on coal for heat, Helen enjoyed the atmosphere that burning wood provided for entertaining in the front rooms. The servants had proven diligent in keeping the fires tended. She enjoyed listening to the occasional burst of sound. Every now and again a log would succumb to the flames, falling with a thud as it broke into smaller pieces. Helen was right; the scent of wood burning did indeed add a level of interest and comfort to the atmosphere. She would miss the fire come summer, as well as the chance to enjoy it in such glorious company.

In the meantime, she looked across the lace-covered tea table at her companion. Lord Brunswick's lips were down-turned, a contrast from the delightful expression he had worn the previous night. Even in his less-than-enchanting mood, he was ever so appealing. She discovered a sudden and urgent yearning to please him.

"I doubt he was any more fascinating than you will prove to be," Dorothea assured him. "Judging from my conversation with you last night, I look forward to a delightful teatime with you."

Her words encouraged his smile to return. "And I with you."

Studying him, Dorothea realized that even if he uttered

not a word during their entire visit, she would still prefer him to Hans. Stratford's brand of attractiveness held a greater appeal for her than did Hans's even though Hans was hardly homely. But Stratford possessed an even more appealing quality that Hans missed—a highly developed spiritual life. Stratford spoke of sacred matters and his relationship with the Lord in an easy and natural manner that indicated he was comfortable with this part of his life and that it was a large part of his identity. Hans, on the other hand, kept his conversation focused on himself. The contrast put Stratford far and above Hans in every way.

"You must tell me something." He studied the portrait hanging over the fireplace mantel. "Who is that lovely woman?"

"That is Grandmother Witherspoon. I always admired that portrait when it hung in her house, and I am glad Helen is enjoying it now. See how the artist captured her expression? I feel that she could come alive and step right into this room with us at any moment." Dorothea shared a few more insights about art, and they talked about some of their favorite paintings. She enjoyed Stratford's knowledge of and enthusiasm for the subject.

After a time, Stratford's gaze returned to Grandmother Witherspoon's portrait. "She really was a beautiful woman. She reminds me so much of you."

"Does she?" Dorothea regarded the figure's eyes, the curve of her face, and her slim but womanly frame. "Yes, I suppose she does look a bit like I do. I certainly take your observation as a supreme compliment."

He studied the picture. "I would think the lady in the portrait would be equally pleased by the comparison."

"I would like to think so, although I never knew my grandmother. From all accounts, she was quite the prim and proper lady, God rest her soul." Dorothea couldn't resist sharing a bit more. What could telling a little story hurt? "This is a secret just between us, but I understand she occasionally imbibed in a pinch of snuff when she thought no one was watching."

"Did she?" Lord Brunswick laughed. Dorothea liked the way he expressed his mirth freely, without reservation. "How amusing. I must say, I have a fine lineage of ancestors who had their share of oddities, as well. Would you like to hear about them?"

"Oh, yes indeed."

Lord Brunswick's amusing accounts kept her laughing the rest of the afternoon away, even more than she had with Hans. She found the conversation doubly stimulating since she could participate rather than simply providing an audience for someone's tales, however fascinating.

Even better, she discovered that her guess formed the previous evening was correct—that Stratford really did seek to walk with the Lord. In such times, a devout man was a treasure indeed. Perhaps she was not such a poor judge of character as Helen had tried to claim.

By the end of their time together, she was addressing him by his Christian name. *Stratford*. The name rolled off her tongue as easily as her own.

Before she realized how much time had passed, the flat *bang* of the gong summoned them to dinner.

"Dinner already?" Stratford consulted his pocket watch. "Why, indeed it is. I have certainly overstayed my welcome." He rose from his seat.

She followed his example. "Not at all. Why, I would not have known it was the dinner hour myself had the gong not sounded. Will you not stay and dine with us?"

"Oh, I really cannot impose."

"Come now. Is your cook really better than Helen's?" she teased.

"I doubt it. Perhaps I should find out." He smiled in a way that told her that he wanted to learn more than how Helen's cook prepared roast of beef.

Dorothea felt just the tiniest bit of remorse upon inviting

Stratford without asking Helen first. Then she looked at Stratford, so dashing in a dark suit that fit his fine form to perfection, his blue eyes seldom taking their gaze from her face, his mouth that tempted her to dream about a kiss. . . .

She quickly tamped down any regrets and held her head high as she walked into the dining hall with Stratford by her side. Helen and Luke had already been seated, though Luke rose in deference to the fact that a lady had entered the room. Helen's eyebrows arched in question, but she greeted Stratford in a cordial manner, as did Luke.

Dorothea posed her query. "Helen, because of the advanced hour, I have asked Lord Brunswick to dine with us. I know you do not mind in the least."

If Helen minded, she recovered in record speed. "Indeed not. I am delighted to have a dinner guest." She motioned to the maid to set an extra plate.

Luke didn't seem to mind the extra company, either. The two men established a quick rapport that Dorothea knew reflected the comfort of an established acquaintanceship. Even Helen didn't seem to mind conversing with him. In light of Helen's stated preference for Hans earlier, by meal's end Dorothea considered the event to be a victory.

"Try not to be a stranger, Brunswick," Luke encouraged him after dinner. "I did tell you about the hunt we have planned for the weekend?"

"I believe it was mentioned in passing, though I was not aware I was to be included."

"Of course you are."

"Then you can count on me to join you." He sent Dorothea a sidelong glance. "I might even pay a call before then, by your leave."

Luke answered. "Never give a second thought to dropping in on us. You are always welcome here."

Dorothea wished Helen would concur, but since Luke spoke for the members of his household, she knew Stratford could feel comfortable visiting as he liked.

Stratford bid Dorothea a proper adieu. By the time his feet hit the stoop and the door shut behind him, she nearly felt like collapsing with exhaustion and excitement.

"Well," Helen noted, "I never would have believed I would one day be juggling two men practically tripping over each other in the foyer."

"Have you been married to me so long that you are envious, my dear?" Luke gave her a reassuring peck on the cheek.

"I enjoyed my courting days, but I do not wish for them to return. Indeed, I am much too happy now." The sparkle in Helen's eyes as she regarded Luke said she told the truth.

"And I return those feelings a hundredfold." Luke's smile mirrored his wife's. "I shall leave you to your talk of delicate ladylike matters while I retire to the drawing room for a cigar. By your leave, ladies?"

"Certainly," Dorothea said.

"Do enjoy," Helen added.

Dorothea must have had a dreamy look in her own eyes, for Helen set her back into reality as soon as her husband was out of earshot. "Really, Dorothea, must you encourage that man?"

"I assume you mean Lord Brunswick?"

"Yes. Why would you flirt with him so openly when you have more than piqued the interest of Baron von Lunenburg? Remember how much you owe him."

"Yes." Through force of will Dorothea managed not to cringe. She almost wished she hadn't accepted the favor, since Helen never seemed to miss a chance to remind her about her debt of gratitude. "And I returned the favor by giving him a most attentive ear all afternoon."

"I have a feeling that being in his company was not a form of torture."

"I cannot say it was."

"I am amazed," Helen said, "by how much attention you have attracted considering you have no dowry to offer. I wonder if Lord Brunswick is aware of your financial situation?"

Dorothea swallowed. She had been so entranced by

Stratford that she hadn't considered how little she had to offer him in the way of money. Would he lose all interest in her once he found out she had no dowry?

"You should be down on your knees thanking Providence that Baron von Lunenburg likes a pretty face." Warning filled Helen's voice.

"And you think Lord Brunswick is a pauper?"

"No. I would not say he is."

"Then perchance he will be content with what you call a pretty face, as well, then. Unlike most of the other men we know, Stratford is a devoted Christian."

"Stratford?" Helen inquired. "So now you are calling him by his Christian name?"

"He granted me leave, yes. And I have the distinct impression that money is not his primary concern." Dorothea decided to play a trump card. "And you noticed how Luke talks easily to him, and he encouraged him to return. Obviously he approves."

"Luke is not the one who may marry him."

"Helen, I appreciate your concern, but no one is anywhere near the point of making such a declaration. We have only known each other a short while, and my time here is limited. I merely plan to enjoy what pleasant company comes my way before I must return to my new life in London."

And uncertainty. And a dreary room. And hope for a paying position suitable for a lady.

"I assure you," Dorothea told Helen, "Baron von Lunenburg has my undying gratitude for getting me out of debt. And I will always show him the utmost deference. But taking him on as a suitor? Why, even if that had been my plan, he never stated his intentions."

"Perhaps granting you such a large favor was a way of stating his intentions."

"Then he had best speak in plain language. As you well know by now, I have never been good at playing games."

"But, my dear, games are so much fun."

six

Stratford whistled as he rode home. What a wonderful afternoon he had spent with Dorothea, a more lovely time than he had experienced in recent memory. Whenever images of that snake Lunenburg popped into his head, he shook them out of his mind. Even though she and Lunenburg had been engaged in animated conversation when Stratford arrived, Dorothea had assured him with both actions and words that she preferred his company.

Of course she was being courteous to Lunenburg by continuing to grant him the pleasure of her company. She thought he had paid her way. Perhaps Lunenburg was right. Perhaps Stratford was a fool for letting the man take credit for his good deed. Yet the verse that spurred Stratford spun around in his mind: *"But when thou doest alms, let not thy left hand know what thy right hand doeth: that thine alms may be in secret: and thy Father which seeth in secret himself shall reward thee openly."*

What if Dorothea found out he, not Lunenburg, was her benefactor? Would she treat him with the same deference? And what if she did? Would her attention be motivated by gratitude alone?

No, he wouldn't want polite company as a reward from a grateful woman. He wanted the type of natural companionship he had enjoyed with her this afternoon. Better yet, he wanted Dorothea to love him for himself. The idea that he was hiding behind scripture to conceal his real motive for paying her debts disturbed him, yet he could think of no other way. He had to establish a relationship with her before she found out so she wouldn't think he pitied her.

Heavenly Father, forgive me. And if Dorothea hates me when she learns the truth—which is bound to happen—let her forgive me, too.

The thought of her departure, scheduled to take place in less than a fortnight, left him with a feeling of dread. He had to think of a way to keep her in the country. But how? If only he had a position open in his household that would be worthy of a woman of her station. But he did not. Despite Dorothea's determination to make her own way, Stratford thought that taking on the role of a governess—an option she considered—was beneath her. Not that he had children for her to tutor.

He arrived at his home and dismounted, handing over his faithful white steed to a stable boy. Then he remembered part of the conversation he had just shared with Dorothea. Something she had said gave him an idea. He dismissed any lingering doubts and called the stable boy to bring back his horse. He had to return to the Syms estate without further ado.

❧

Dorothea looked out of the window when she heard the sound of horse's hooves approaching the estate. "Who might that be at this late hour?"

"Surely it is not yet another caller," Helen speculated.

Dorothea recognized Stratford returning. "Why, our visitor is Stratford!"

Helen strode up beside Dorothea and peered outside. "I think you are right. Strange. He was here nearly the entire afternoon and evening. What else could he possibly have to say?"

"Maybe he left his coat or hat here? Although I was certain he was wearing both when he left."

"Whatever his business is, it must be important. He is riding as though his life depended upon it."

"By your leave, I would like to greet him at the door and find out for myself," Dorothea said.

"Dorothea! Must you be so forward?"

"I promise not to say anything shameful."

Their conversation soon became moot as the butler

answered, then announced Stratford's arrival and request to see Dorothea.

Helen whispered, "I think you should say you are indisposed. If you are always available, you will look too eager."

"That might be good advice for the coy woman, but since Stratford looked as though his business was urgent, I shall see him." Seeing Helen roll her glance to the ceiling and back, Dorothea added, "Maybe I will be indisposed next time."

He was standing near the fire, which had burned down to a few glowing embers when she entered the drawing room. He nodded to her. "Good evening."

"Good evening. I did not expect to see you again so soon." She smiled in return and chose a comfortable chair in which to seat herself.

He sat on the sofa. "Truth be told, neither did I. But I had to see you. My business is too urgent to wait. It concerns our conversation today."

"Oh, that." She pondered what he could have regretted revealing to her. "Are you remorseful about telling me about how your second cousin was a spy for the American colonists during the revolt? I promise I will never say a word. Not even to Helen."

"I have no fear that you would ever break a confidence. No, I am here about another part of our conversation. You mentioned you enjoy painting."

"Yes, I do. Very much."

"I should have thought to inquire earlier, but since I did not, I shall ask now, by your leave. I was wondering if I might be able to view some of your work?"

She felt her smile vanish. "If only you could. I would be more than happy for you to look at my paintings, except that I did not bring any with me."

Stratford's mouth curled into a disappointed line. "Of course. What possessed me?" His shoulders slumped.

"Even if I had the inclination to bring some of my

pictures from London, it would have been impossible. I sold everything I ever painted."

His eyes rounded. "Indeed?"

"Not intentionally, mind you. I did not seek to charge a fee for my little hobby. My friends merely granted me a little pocket money as a courtesy." She clasped her hands. "I would not be entirely honest if I did not admit that I did keep two small pieces, but they are not really my best work."

"I care not. I still want to see them. May I?"

"Very well. I have them in my bedchamber. Would you wait while I retrieve them?"

"Of course."

Dorothea hurried about her task so as not to keep him lingering alone any longer than necessary. The paintings were held up by small easels positioned on a shelf in her room, a constant reminder of the parents she would always love.

Soon she brought two small paintings for his perusal. She found him still sitting on the upholstered sofa and took a seat beside him so she could present him with her work. "This is Mother." She showed him a painting of a woman with light hair like her own and mysterious brown eyes.

"Beautiful," he said.

"My work or my mother?" she teased.

"Both." He extended his hand for the second painting.

"This is Father."

She watched Stratford study the portrait of a distinguished-looking gentleman with dark hair that had grayed at the temples. "A handsome fellow. No surprise." He smiled at Dorothea.

"Since they were my own dear parents, I hope you will not think me vain to observe that they were pleasing subjects to paint."

"In my judgment, you do not exaggerate. I would say that based on this work you could compliment the most difficult subject."

"You flatter me."

"I do not speak in hyperbole. These are astounding." He kept his eyes on the pictures. "Why, they are just as good, if not better, than most of the professional portraits I see."

"Thank you. I wonder about the artists to whom you compare me?"

"Talented artists. One in particular. William Amory was our local portrait painter for a time. He was also our doctor."

She tried to remember the people she had met. "I recall meeting Dr. Oliver but not Dr. Amory."

"I am surprised the Amory name does not register with you. He married your cousin Lavonia Penn."

"Lavonia Penn." She searched her memory for details to place with the name. "Oh, yes. Of course. Lavonia is Helen's cousin from another branch of the family. I do remember Helen writing to us that Lavonia came to stay with her for a time, and that is when she met Dr. Amory. They have since moved to America to practice medicine among the poor."

"Yes, you have the details right."

"I do admire them so. I would never think of moving to such a savage place."

"One must go where he is called." Stratford remembered someone else. "I remember attending Kitty's wedding to the vicar. How is she now?"

"Enjoying life in the parish where he was transferred, as far as I know."

Stratford grinned. "I do seem to remember he wanted to advance in his profession."

"Yes, the Lord has granted him career success, but they have no children as of yet," Dorothea added, even though Stratford hadn't made a specific inquiry.

"Children. Do I see dreams in your eyes?"

She squirmed. What could she say? "Does not every woman dream of children once she is married?" She felt a desperate need to deflect attention from herself, lest Stratford think her too forward. "And does not every man dream of being a father?"

"I do. One day."

"One day."

He made a show of studying the portraits. "I beg your pardon, I did not intend to allow my conversation to wander so far off the presentation of my idea to you."

As much as she felt thrilled to learn that they shared such an important dream, Dorothea knew that Stratford made a wise move to steer the conversation to safer waters. "Idea?"

"Yes. You have made clear to me that you are determined to make your way in the world instead of depending on the kindness of distant relations."

"I have not wavered, and I never will."

"Then you will find my suggestion intriguing. In the absence of Dr. Amory, we have not had a portrait painter here." He looked into her eyes. His expression was not the rapt one of a suitor but the straightforward guise of a businessman. "Dorothea, have you ever considered painting portraits on commission? People are eager for their likenesses to be painted, and from the looks of these, you are quite good. I can only assume you have taken a good number of lessons and learned the craft well."

"Yes, I was allowed to pursue my little hobby under the guidance of a master of the arts in finishing school, Monsieur Journeu. He encouraged me, but I thought he was just prodding me as any good teacher would." She thought back to after she graduated. "Later, my friends were kind enough to humor me by making a few purchases, but I really do not think I am that good."

"I do not see how you can look at these and come to that conclusion. The modesty of a lady becomes you, I must say. But when business is in question, reticence must be abandoned for accurate representation of your talent," he told her.

"Business?"

"Yes. I believe you are an exquisite artist. In fact, let me prove it. If you will agree, I would like to commission you to paint a portrait of me."

"Really?'

"Yes. I can write you a bank draft today. How does fifty pounds sound for a retainer fee?"

"Fifty pounds! I have never been paid nearly so much."

"Then your friends got a bargain."

"But fifty pounds!"

"And fifty more will be forthcoming once the work is complete."

"Really, Stratford, you do not have to buy my friendship."

"I would hope not. If you were a man, I would tell you that I was insulted that you would make such an observation."

Dorothea felt a wave of remorse even though she thought Stratford overreacted to her remark. "I am so sorry. Please, I beg your deepest indulgence. I never meant to say that. I simply do not wish you to overpay me out of some sort of misplaced obligation of friendship."

"I am not, I assure you," he said. "It so happens that I do not believe in the concept of the starving artist. Please. Allow me to be your first patron here in the country. I promise you once people see my portrait, you will gain even more clients."

Dorothea mulled over his offer. If she took the commission, the job would allow her to remain in the country. She wouldn't have to go back to London after all. "I will need to ask Helen's opinion in this matter."

"I have no doubt she will be agreeable to the idea."

Dorothea remembered her cousin's promise never to abandon her. And the idea of starting a business painting portraits—a hobby she enjoyed—held much more appeal than becoming a governess or nanny ever could for her.

"You know, I think you are quite right. And if I can build up a business as an artist, I can either pay my way here or move to my own place." She looked at the wainscoted ceiling. "Not somewhere this large or luxurious, of course. But somewhere." The idea sounded agreeable.

"Good. It is settled, then. Consider yourself Lady Dorothea Witherspoon, *Artiste!*"

ప

A month later, Dorothea studied the emerging portrait of Stratford. She was in the process of painting a few more strokes to complete the work, not a difficult task even though her sitting with Stratford was complete for the day. When she first began painting his picture, she hadn't thought she could ever capture his exquisite likeness, but somehow, through the grace of God, she had almost managed to show him as comely in the painting as he appeared in real life.

Helen entered and looked over Dorothea's shoulder. "That painting is absolutely exquisite. It certainly flatters its subject."

She touched up a spot on the black suit he wore in the picture. "Do you really think it flatters him? I think it looks just like him."

"Then you must be in love."

Love. Really? Dorothea wondered. Stratford had certainly seemed more than companionable during their sessions. To her delight, they had fallen into the habit of prolonging their visits after each portrait sitting. Though she had anticipated attending worship since childhood, his presence each Sunday now pressed her into even more eager attendance. But to enter into any irrevocable entanglement too early was something she wanted to avoid.

"A confession is not necessary. I can see the love in your eyes," Helen proclaimed.

"I did not come here to find a husband, if that is what you imply." Dorothea kept her gaze on the portrait.

Helen scrutinized her. "I would not believe every woman who tried to tell me such a tale, but I do believe you. You are much too honest for your own good."

She touched her brush in a dab of black paint. "Can one really be too honest for one's own good?"

Helen shrugged. "I do not suppose I could prove my theory by you. Luck seems to follow you into the best of circumstances."

"Speaking of which, I do wish you would let me repay you for allowing me to remain here while I paint Stratford's portrait."

"A small gesture, especially compared to the sum of ten thousand pounds."

Dorothea flinched.

"I am sorry. I did not mean that. Of course I am delighted to have you here. Perhaps you might consent to painting my portrait, as well." She crossed her arms and admired the painting. "Although I do have a better assignment for you first. Why not offer to paint Baron von Lunenburg's portrait?"

Such a notion had never occurred to Dorothea, but under the circumstances, she didn't think the idea could be considered unreasonable. "Do you really think I should?"

"Indeed. And," Helen added, "such a plan encourages him to court you."

Dorothea held back an exasperated breath. "But you just said I love Stratford."

"Love is all well and good, but the best match is the thing for which you should strive."

She knew which man Helen meant. The best match indeed.

☙

The village bustled as Stratford went about his errands. He wished he had sent a servant to town instead, but personal business demanded he go himself.

Ready for a break, Stratford headed toward the tavern. An appealing smell of cooking meat rolled into the street as a customer exited and held the door open for him. Yes, a hearty bowl of beef stew and a slice or two of buttered bread would do the trick.

Since so many people sought refuge from icy rain and cold, Stratford wasn't surprised to see the tavern filled with people. In fact, considering the welcome heat he felt as soon as he crossed the threshold, the idea of finding warmth there seemed like sound judgment. Voices—mainly male, since few women would care to brave the elements—carried on many conversations, filling the room with the sounds of conviviality. The smell of baking bread dominated the odors of meats, vegetables, and pastries that mixed with the yeasty odor of ale and the bitter scent of brewed coffee and tea.

He surveyed the inside to see if he knew anyone and saw Lunenburg sitting with Lord Hampton at a table in the center of the room. Suddenly the idea of stew and bread—and even warmth for his chilled body—didn't seem so urgent. He turned to leave.

"Brunswick, old man!" Lunenburg called, "Come sit with us."

Too late.

Stratford held back a grimace. Seeing no way to retreat without appearing unsociable, he stepped to their table and took a seat. "Good afternoon, gentlemen. It is a pleasure to see you both," he said amid their greetings.

"You are lucky we happened to be here." With an exaggerated motion, Lunenburg made a point of surveying the room. "Otherwise, you would have encountered difficulty in finding a place to sit at all."

"Yes, thank you." Stratford pushed back one of the wooden chairs and situated himself in it. The legs made a scratching sound against the wide floor planks as he pulled up to the sturdy pine table. "I cannot stay long."

"I do not see why not," Lunenburg said. "Dorothea has almost finished your portrait."

He bristled. "And how would you know that?"

"Because she has just commissioned my portrait." Lunenburg snapped his fingers at a serving girl. "Will you be drinking ale with us, Brunswick?"

"I prefer hot tea, thank you."

"Why am I not surprised?" Lunenburg sent a disapproving glance up to the ceiling and ordered tea. " 'Monk' would be a fine nickname for Brunswick, wouldn't you agree, Hampton?"

The other man laughed, but Stratford failed to see the

humor. "One cup of hot tea will do more to warm you up on a frigid day like this than a gallon of ale ever could."

"After a gallon of ale, would one care about the weather?" Lunenburg asked. "Not unlike when one is in the company of a beautiful woman. Such as Lady Dorothea."

"Dorothea. Yes," Stratford said. "So you commissioned a portrait with her? I was not aware that you knew she possesses a talent for painting portraits."

"How could he not know?" Hampton leaned over so that his expansive belly touched the edge of the table. "Everyone in the parish has heard Helen rave over the image she painted of you. Says it flatters you greatly."

"She would think that," Stratford muttered under his breath.

Hampton leaned back and rubbed his belly. "I think I might have her paint my portrait, as well."

"And take off a few pounds for you, eh, Hampton?" Lunenburg laughed, and Hampton joined him in his mirth.

Stratford allowed himself a half smile as a serving girl placed a cup of tea before him. Only Lunenburg could get away with such truthful jesting. Hampton would have chastised anyone else.

"She has even offered to paint it for nothing," Lunenburg bragged.

"For nothing?" Hampton took in a breath. "Why?"

Lunenburg shrugged but refused to make eye contact with Stratford. "I suppose it's her way of letting people know she paints and paints well."

"Was your portrait free, Brunswick?" Hampton leaned toward him.

"No. In fact, I am the one who encouraged her to paint portraits, and I voluntarily offered her a grand sum for mine." He gave Lunenburg a pointed look. "I did not feel I should ask her for charity."

Lunenburg's inability to meet Stratford's gaze told him that he understood the underlying message. "Well, yes, of

seven

"I received another commission for a portrait today," Dorothea told Helen as they sat by the fire in the drawing room over their sewing a month later. Spring had arrived, and with it, less necessity for a fire, although a small one kept them in comfort against the season's brisk chill.

Helen looked up from the napkin she was embroidering. "Wonderful! You should be proud of your little hobby."

Dorothea ran a thread through one of her night shifts to repair a hem that had begun to fray. "Lady Cheatham and her two daughters. They want a group portrait."

"That is excellent! Why, with their commission and Lord Hampton's, your pastime is bringing you quite a bit of pocket money." By now Dorothea had learned just how much Helen's voice lilted when she was truly impressed. Her voice lilted that way now. "I admire your talent, I must say."

"Thank you." Dorothea paused for a moment, savoring Helen's kind words. "I have been blessed. I thank the Lord every day and night for His mercy, for allowing me to progress beyond my wildest imaginings from where I was in my life when I first came here to ask you to help me. And I will never be able to thank you enough, either." She inspected her work. "I will be most sorry when I leave you soon. I will miss you terribly."

Helen dropped a stitch. "Whatever makes you think I want you to leave?"

"I have taken advantage of your kind hospitality long enough, although of course I do enjoy your home and company very much."

"And we, yours. I will not hear of any cousin of mine living by herself when I have this beautiful estate and so much room for you here. I insist that you stay with us," Helen instructed.

"But—"

"But nothing. Besides, will you not be wed to one of our local bachelors soon? I noticed even Lord Hampton taking notice of you, and when he comes to sit for you, I do not believe he thinks only of his portrait."

She visualized the pompous and portly Lord Hampton. "I cannot imagine myself as Lady Hampton. And I am in no hurry to wed."

Helen resumed her sewing. "Do not vex yourself. Baron von Lunenburg will be making a declaration soon enough, I daresay."

Dorothea didn't answer. She didn't want any promise from the man Helen had chosen for her. Her heart remained with Stratford.

❧

As Stratford sat in St. Mark's Church, he studied the back of Lunenburg's head above the worn but polished wooden pew in front of him. Even though Dorothea continued to worship beside him rather than Lunenburg, he couldn't help but envy the man the time he spent with Dorothea as he had his portrait painted.

At that moment, she sent him a sideways smile, which he returned. Did she share the same type of rapport with Lunenburg? Stratford was aware from tidbits of gossip he had overheard and from his general demeanor that Lunenburg wanted everyone to think so.

Stratford gave himself a mental whipping. Why couldn't he simply declare his feelings to Dorothea? Feelings that had grown from fondness to love.

Because of his secret, that's why.

She seemed to return his feelings, but what would happen if he told her he was her benefactor? Those sentiments were sure to go from fondness to mere gratitude. He didn't want gratitude. Such an emotion was noble but nothing on which to base a lifelong union.

Stratford never regretted paying off Dorothea's debts. Once the burden was lifted, she had blossomed from a fearful girl standing all alone in Helen's foyer to a confident and happy woman. Because of Stratford's secret largesse and open encouragement, she had been lifted from an existence filled with worry to a life full of creative energy. And she would never realize just how much of a role he had played. Instead, he let that scoundrel, Lunenburg, take all the credit—and paid him for the privilege. And all because he had been trying to follow scripture.

Were Christians really supposed to feel so foolish when they were doing their best? He wondered.

Perhaps he should tell her the truth the next time he paid her a call. He gave her a sideways glance. No. She would think he pitied her. Nothing could have been further from the truth.

Father in heaven, I pray I am doing the right thing not to tell Dorothea.

The sense of peace he felt told him that surely he was doing right by Dorothea and himself.

❧

Hours later, after Stratford had taken Sunday dinner at the Syms estate as had become his habit, he made his way home. Sleepy, he anticipated a nap to help him digest the slab of roast mutton and gravy, potatoes, mixed vegetables, two slices of liberally buttered bread, and not one, but two, blueberry preserve tarts. He always tended to overeat whenever he dined at the Syms estate, a habit he had to break.

He resolved to break that habit the following Sunday.

As Stratford rode his horse up the drive to his estate, he noticed a strange carriage parked in front. Who could be visiting him?

His butler greeted him at the door. "Gilbert Meara, Esquire, is waiting for you in the drawing room, sir." He handed him Gilbert's card.

"Gilbert! What is he doing here?" Stratford returned

his attention to the butler. "Did you make sure he had refreshment?"

"I was aware that Mr. Meara was no stranger to you, so I offered hospitality. I instructed Cook to prepare a light lunch and tea, sir."

"Very good. Bring us more tea, if you will."

"Yes, sir."

Stratford didn't delay in going to see his friend. "Gilbert! To what do I owe the pleasure of your visit?"

"Clearly I have taken you by surprise." As they exchanged a hearty handshake and pats on the back, Gilbert quipped, "Might I ask you how you could have forgotten all about me?"

"Forgotten you?"

"Yes. I told you I would take you up on your offer for a stay here once I had a break in my legal caseload. I went to a lot of trouble to clear my schedule this month, but I did just that, as I promised."

"Yes, I do remember now. And I am glad you decided to make the trip." Since he felt like a fool for forgetting he had extended the invitation, Stratford hoped his hearty welcome made up for his lack of attention to such details.

"Hmm. You would have remembered in the old days. I suppose something—or someone—has caused you to become forgetful?"

Stratford chuckled. "You know me too well. I was at church, and then I dined at the Syms estate."

"The Syms estate. I never heard you mention an eligible lady residing there since Lavonia Penn visited some time ago."

"Must an eligible lady be present for me to dine at someone else's house?"

"I suppose not, but I cannot think of a better reason, can you?"

Stratford chuckled.

Gilbert continued, "Perhaps she—whoever she is—will make up for the dull morning you no doubt spent in church."

"I spent the morning in church, yes, but I would not call worship dull."

"To each his own," Gilbert answered. "Perhaps I should have been occupying a pew myself. But you know me and religion; the two of us have never gotten on."

Stratford refrained from shaking his head. Gilbert and he had been friends since childhood. Though as boys they had been acolytes together, leading the processional for worship each Sunday, Gilbert had always found church boring. As an adult, he became a devotee of the reason and rationality behind Enlightenment ideas and then abandoned any pretext of being a Christian. Stratford would not have chosen Gilbert as a friend had they met as adults, yet Gilbert remained a decent man, and Stratford kept him in his prayers, that he would be protected by God and would return to His church.

Rather than sharing this information and risking Gilbert's embarrassment, Stratford chose a quip more suited to Gilbert's liking. "Still the heathen after all this time?"

"I have not wavered yet, but during my visit I know you will do your best to make me love faith over reason. So I will not be staying long."

"If you are that fearful of being present in my house, then you must be wavering at least a little."

"Well, there is this woman I met. She insists that I should go to church."

"Then there may be hope for you yet." Stratford kept his voice teasing. "So tell me about her."

They caught up on each other's lives through the afternoon, conversing as though only days rather than months had passed since their last visit. As they lingered over a treat of white cake topped with an icing of a stewed fruit mixture, Stratford told him about Dorothea.

"She sounds quite lovely in all respects," Gilbert said. "Do you think you might convince her to become your wife?"

"I admit the idea has crossed my mind, but I have not made a definite move yet."

"Why not?"

Stratford debated as to whether or not he should reveal the whole story to his friend. He decided that sharing the details with Gilbert might offer him a new perspective, one from someone who could offer the objective opinion and understanding of a friend.

Gilbert contemplated Stratford's reasoning and situation. "I can see your viewpoint and why you decided to keep your benevolence a secret from her. But I think the time to tell all is drawing near. If, after all this time, her opinion of you changes, then you can take it as a sign from your God that she is not the person for you. And you can content yourself with the knowledge that you helped another Christian rise above a dire situation that was created through no fault or crime of her own."

Stratford set his empty dessert plate on the table beside the wing chair. "Thank you. Your opinion has set my mind at ease. I shall now look for the right time to tell her. I know not when that time will be, but I sense I will feel led when it arrives."

A servant entered and added a large log to the fire. The two men watched him. Stratford could see from Gilbert's expression that he was immersed in thought. He had some thinking of his own to do.

As the servant finished his task, Stratford ventured onto a new topic. "You said you wanted to commission a portrait at some point."

"I did, but I never took action beyond talking about it. I thought a nice portrait might decorate the front room of my office well or offer a fine addition to my own drawing room."

"Why delay? You are as handsome now as you ever will be."

"I see you are not above using flattery to convince me. So who is this fine man you want me to patronize? A vicar in need of a few extra crowns to feed a brood of orphaned children?"

Stratford chuckled. "Not exactly. But this artist is quite

good. Would you like to see proof?"

"Why not?"

Stratford stood. "Then tag along with me."

Gilbert followed Stratford into the library, where his barely dry portrait hung over the fireplace mantel.

"Forgive the chill, Gilbert. I had not planned on spending any time in this room today."

"That is quite all right."

Stratford didn't have to point out the picture's location to his friend. The portrait loomed large in the room. He noticed that Gilbert's eyes caught a glimpse of the painting immediately.

Gilbert whistled. "That is certainly a fine piece of artwork. The detail is such that I can read the letter *B* on your signet ring with no trouble at all."

"You are not the first one to notice the fine attention to detail. It is one aspect that distinguishes passable artwork from the superb, would you not agree?"

"Indeed. But why relegate such a fine likeness to obscurity here? Why not place it in the drawing room where everyone will see it?"

"I will one day. But I am loath to replace my mother's portrait that hangs over the mantel there now, God rest her soul."

Gilbert nodded. "I understand that sentiment completely."

Stratford watched his friend study the painting. "Some like to say that picture flatters me."

Gilbert looked at Stratford, then back at the portrait, then back again. "I would say it looks just like you."

"Thank you."

Gilbert continued to study the image, rubbing his clean-shaven chin with his fingers. "If I did not know better, I would also say the artist has developed quite a fondness for you."

Stratford startled. "Indeed? Why?"

"The picture has a spark that shows a unique partiality to its subject. Can you not see it?"

"I—I had not thought about it. I just know I do like the picture very much."

"So you should. Too bad your artist is a man."

Stratford laughed and welcomed the opportunity to deflect the conversation from himself. "A man of your wit should know better than to make such broad assumptions. In fact, the artist is a lady."

"A lady?" He studied the portrait again. "My, but she is quite good. I did not think a woman would have access to the type of training required to learn how to paint in such a fine manner."

"She attended a finishing school suitable for her station." Stratford regarded the painting himself. "And I do believe she possesses a degree of natural talent."

"True. Any determined student can learn proper strokes, but genius is needed to bring out the passion that exists in a picture such as this one. So who is our talented member of the fairer sex?"

"Lady Dorothea Witherspoon."

"The lady you have been telling me about all this time? I might have known." One of Gilbert's eyebrows raised itself above the other. "So why not marry her instead of encouraging others to sit for her? You can trust me, but not every man will put aside the opportunity to charm the lady. Or is that why you asked me to sit for her? Because you know I would never pursue the object of your affections?"

"Obviously I do not possess the sly wit that you do, Gilbert, because the issue of trust never entered my mind. I can trust Dorothea."

"So you say, but what of the men?"

"If another man woos her away, then I will know that she was not fit to be my wife, and I would consider such a discovery now rather than later a favor from the Lord. In the meantime, I will have you to know that she possesses an admirably independent spirit and is taking portrait commissions in an effort to regain financial stability." Stratford hastened to add, "She has paid mighty consequences for her father's sins. I will not reveal the details, but she has sacrificed greatly to pay off his debts. Debts she did not incur herself."

"And you want your friends to buy this lady's work in order to help recover her fortune."

"Something like that. But she is truly talented, as you can plainly see. If that were not so, I would not ask you to commission a portrait with her," Stratford assured him. "She even told me she has sold everything she has ever painted. The only pictures she kept for herself are likenesses of her departed parents, God rest their souls."

"I can see why people clamor for her work." Gilbert nodded. "Judging from this image, and the fact that you recommend her so highly, I have decided I will gladly contribute to the increase of her fortune in return for a fine portrait of myself. Not that I think the picture she renders of me will bespeak as much passion."

The butler chose that moment to interrupt to present a missive. Stratford excused himself long enough to read its contents. "Ah, we have an invitation for Tuesday evening."

"We do? I had no idea anyone would know I was visiting the country."

"I admit *we* do not have an invitation, but *I* do. And since you are my guest here in my home, that means *we* do."

"But I cannot impose."

"Of course you can. For you see, it is for dinner at the home where Dorothea is staying. I know the host well. They will not mind at all if I write to them and ask to include you."

"Considering how you rave over the cuisine you enjoy at the Syms estate, I would be most grateful. And I do look forward to meeting Lady Witherspoon."

❧

On Tuesday evening, true to his word, after gaining permission from Luke, Stratford took Gilbert along with him to dine at Helen's. What he hadn't been expecting were more guests.

And when he spotted Lunenburg among them, anticipation turned to disappointment.

"Well," Lunenburg addressed Gilbert a tad too loudly, "I see we have someone new here. My, but the country is attracting all sorts of new people lately. I do not believe I have had the pleasure, Lord. . . ?"

"Gilbert Meara, Esquire," he answered.

As formal introductions proceeded, Stratford noticed that his friend's lips had pursed themselves into a thin line. His eyes took on a hard glint when he looked at Lunenburg. Gilbert was no fool, but surely he couldn't discern a man's character just by looking at his face. Yet he could see by the way Gilbert stared at him that something about Lunenburg disturbed him. Something was amiss.

Stratford had no time to ponder the thought further as he discovered to his pleasure that he was seated by Dorothea. He wondered if she had contrived the arrangement and if she was the one responsible for his inclusion in the dinner.

Helen had invited a couple of other ladies to even out her table. Noticing this, Stratford made sure to thank her doubly for allowing him to include his friend at the last moment. Helen, ever the gracious hostess, professed she didn't mind. After consideration, Stratford surmised she was likely not fibbing. Both of the extra women were nearing the age whereupon if they didn't make a match soon, they were doomed forever to spinsterhood. Stratford noted that Gilbert played the consummate gentleman by paying close attention to their conversation. He entertained them with witty comments and stories so they laughed often during the evening.

Still, Lunenburg kept everyone at the table—except Stratford—mesmerized. "One would not believe the tremendous investment opportunities awaiting the shrewd man in Africa."

"Africa!" Helen said. "Really?"

"Indeed. The Dark Continent is filled with diamond

mines and gold for those waiting to tap into its rich veins." He leaned so far over that Stratford thought the frill of Lunenburg's shirt would touch his plate soiled with streaks of brown gravy. "Because around this table sit my dearest friends and intimates in the country, I will reveal a great secret to you. Please, I beg of you not to share this confidence with anyone outside of this room. This opportunity is only for you."

"Opportunity?" Luke prodded.

Lunenburg leaned back into his seat. "Yes. My group of investment advisors met just yesterday, and I learned about a new mine that has been recently discovered by our men in the southern part of Africa. Of course, we went to considerable expense to finance their trip. We have plenty of money to keep them afloat in fine style, but if I beg them with enough passion, they just might let you in on what could be the greatest discovery of gold in a hundred years."

Helen sent a look to Luke that reminded Stratford of a dog begging for a bone. "Oh, we must have a part of such an enterprise. We must!"

"Helen, you never need to worry about such affairs," Luke admonished.

"Oh, my, I do beg your pardon," Lunenburg proclaimed. "I am afraid that in my excitement, I have breached etiquette and brought up the dry subject of business in the company of the ladies."

"Oh," one of the spinsters insisted, "but our father will be delighted that we were present to learn about such an opportunity. Might we tell him?"

"Will Lord Bennington take me to task for bending your delicate ears?"

"Not if he can fatten his coffers," the other spinster noted with a chuckle.

"Then by all means, tell him to see me soon. He must hurry before it is too late and all the remaining partnerships are sold."

"Oh, indeed!"

"As for you gentlemen, we can discuss more of the details soon." He eyed each man.

"Can you be more specific?" Luke asked.

"I must speak to my primary partners and get their go-ahead first. I will let you know as soon as I hear from them just how many more investors they are willing to add to their present number."

"Do not delay. Tell us as soon as you know," Luke urged.

Stratford wondered if he was the only person who could see through Lunenburg. He cut a glance to Gilbert, and judging from his blank expression, he had no intention of joining the meeting. Stratford decided to dismiss thoughts of diamonds and gold and spend his attention on Dorothea, who proved to be a delightful companion as always.

Time flew by much too fast. In the twinkling of an eye, the dinner party came to a close and they were bidding each other farewell at the door.

"I shall see you tomorrow for our sitting," Lunenburg made sure to tell Dorothea.

Stratford's stomach turned, but he pushed the feeling away in lieu of something more urgent. "That reminds me, Dorothea," he asked her, "did Gilbert mention how impressed he was by the portrait you painted of me?"

"So impressed that I would like to commission my portrait with you," Gilbert said on cue.

"Oh, how lovely," Helen didn't hesitate to observe.

"So you will be staying here awhile, Mr. Meara?" Dorothea confirmed.

"Yes. Do you have time in your schedule for me? I understand you are quite a popular artist." Gilbert gave Stratford a sideways glance. "Of course, my source is a bit partial."

"Oh, no one can exaggerate her popularity, socially as well as for her artwork," Helen said.

"Really, you do exaggerate," Dorothea protested. "But for a

friend of Stratford's, I will make time."

"Delightful," Gilbert said. "Thank you."

"And I thank you, too." Stratford cast one last longing look Dorothea's way as he ascended into his waiting carriage. He took delight in noticing that she didn't take her gaze from him until he had boarded.

"You really are besotted with her, are you not?" Gilbert asked after the door was shut.

"Such idle talk." Stratford looked outside into the darkness. As they exited, he observed the wrought-iron gate that kept the Syms estate secluded from the outside world and remembered that he needed to contract a craftsman to shore up the mortar on a few places on his own wall.

"Who do you think you are talking to, man?" Gilbert prompted.

Stratford didn't answer.

"Why not make your intentions known before that snake with whom we dined does?"

"Whatever do you mean?" Stratford asked.

"I mean, he was ogling Lady Witherspoon all night, and if you had half an eye you would have noticed." His friend's tone was sharp, obviously meant to bring Stratford to his senses.

"If the snake to whom you refer is Lunenburg, yes, I have an idea."

"Lunenburg. Baron Hans von Lunenburg, right?" Gilbert confirmed.

"Yes."

"What an elegant name he has chosen for himself. I wonder how he managed to concoct it."

"Concoct it? Whatever do you mean?" Stratford asked.

"I mean that Baron Hans von Lunenburg is not who you think he is. He is not a von Lunenburg and certainly not a member of the aristocracy. He is an imposter."

eight

Stratford snapped his attention away from passing trees by the road just outside of the Syms estate. He set his gaze on Gilbert sitting across from him in the carriage. "An imposter? What are you saying?"

"How much more plainspoken can I be? The man you know as Baron von Lunenburg is an imposter, I tell you." Gilbert slapped his knee. The sudden beat emphasized his point.

"Then who is he?"

"I cannot say for certain, which is why I chose not to mention anything at dinner."

"Let me be sure I understand you." Stratford crossed his arms. "You say you know he is an imposter, but you do not know who he is. How can that be?"

"When one is a London solicitor, one is eyewitness to many circumstances." Gilbert leaned toward Stratford, setting his elbows on his thighs and clasping his hands. "Let me tell you one in particular. A few years ago, I was near the courthouse when I saw him being escorted by police. He was in shackles."

"Shackles!" Stratford had trouble picturing the pompous Baron von Lunenburg in shackles. "He was a prisoner? Are you sure?"

"I studied his face as discreetly as I could during the course of the evening. He has aged a bit since then but not too much. The last time I saw him, he was clean-shaven, but he has since grown a mustache, no doubt to help obscure his real identity. And of course at this point in time he wears superb clothing and smells of soap, whereas prison garb and conditions are not quite so fine. But even with all those differences, I have every reason to believe that he and the prisoner I saw are the same."

"What was the criminal's name?"

"That I do not know, either." Gilbert leaned back in the black leather seat.

Stratford couldn't keep his irritation concealed. "You seem to be throwing around many accusations, considering you know next to nothing."

"I can prove my suspicions are true," Gilbert declared. "His name will be easy enough to ascertain. A search of that day's court records will reveal all."

"Surely this man was not so memorable that you can recall the exact day you saw him."

"Believe it or not, he did stick out in my mind," Gilbert said. "I remember feeling sorry for him. He looked so lost and forlorn, like a little boy caught stealing in the nursery—only he was just taking an extra cookie for his dear baby sister who was crying."

"You do have quite the imagination." Stratford chuckled in spite of himself.

"Yes, quite. His expression alone most likely convinced the judge to tread lightly with his sentence," Gilbert observed. "And from all appearances at dinner this evening, his skill at communicating with people has only improved. I can see how he managed to influence so many men in the parish to part with their money."

"And you say you can recall the date you first saw him?"

"Yes. Christmas Eve."

"A time of year when all our senses of compassion are heightened. No wonder you could so easily recall," Stratford reasoned. "Since he showed no recognition of you, I assume he must not have returned your glance."

"No. He kept his eyes averted to the ground."

Stratford could understand why. "I wonder what crime he committed."

"I was not involved in his case, so I have no idea. But for

him to have served his time and been released as a fairly young man, his error must have been minor."

"Or perhaps he was on his way to trial when you spied him, and he was hence found to be innocent."

"That is a distinct possibility. Still, would you trust your friends and loved ones around a former convict—someone even under the slightest suspicion of having committed a crime?"

"Everyone deserves a second chance." Stratford couldn't believe the words coming out of his own mouth in defense of his rival. He suspected the Holy Spirit's prodding played no small role in his attitude.

"You are far too generous," Gilbert's voice assured him from the shadows of the coach.

"Perhaps. But please, tell no one what you know."

"Because you do not trust me?"

"Because I do not trust myself."

"What?"

"Never mind. I will be going to London tomorrow to investigate."

"Good idea, but only if I can go with you. I know more people in the judicial system than you, and I assure you, my connections will be of great assistance."

Since they were nearing the Brunswick estate and the light at the gateway, Stratford could see Gilbert's features well enough to discern that he wore a conspiratorial smile.

"You know me and adventure; we are attracted to each other as a cat is to chasing a mouse."

"What is an intriguing romp to you is a matter of determining a future to me." Stratford revealed through his tone that he felt mixed emotions about the astounding revelation Gilbert had just shared.

"Do not be distressed, old friend. I have a feeling this development will bring you nothing but an improved circumstance and increase the esteem Lady Dorothea holds for you."

"I hope so," Stratford admitted. "All right. I will let

Dorothea know she can begin your portrait sittings upon our return. If I tell her I am going to London on business, it will not be a lie."

Despite his bold assurances, he despised keeping secrets from her. Why did every encounter with Lunenburg seem to result in some sort of deception on his part? Gilbert was right. The sooner he evicted Lunenburg—or whoever he really was—from their lives, the better.

"She need not know the real reason for the trip," Stratford continued aloud. "Not until the time is right."

❧

Clayton Forsythe.

A week later during the return trip from London, the name made the rounds through Stratford's mind. Gilbert had been a tremendous help in making the discovery regarding the real identity of the man they had come to know as Baron Hans von Lunenburg. As they had guessed, Clayton Forsythe had served time in prison for a small crime of thievery, then changed his persona after being released. Using wit and charm, he became a confidence man and made a good enough living from his exploits to pose as a wealthier personage than the one he truly was—a product of the London slums.

According to Gilbert's sources, Clayton experienced close calls with the law, but by the time the authorities had caught up with him at that point, he had befriended a powerful solicitor who managed to keep him out of trouble. According to another friend of Gilbert's, Clayton—who was then posing as Sir Gavin Powell—was warned to leave London or face charges.

After learning this information, Stratford could see why Clayton's next stop had been the country. And no wonder the schemer had taken on a new identity and approached a fresh crowd for money. Stratford could only hope he wasn't too late to keep his friends from losing their money to the conniver.

Stratford had observed Lunenburg. He was good at what

he did. So good that he had already gained the trust of his friends. Even though Stratford had known the men for years, his rivalry with Lunenburg for Dorothea's affections could bring his motives into question. The thought distressed him. Stratford sensed that the conniver relished the sport of love rather than being engaged in serious combat for her heart. He, on the other hand, wanted nothing more than her love. But regardless of each man's motives, the rivalry was too well known by the parish for Stratford to appear to be a disinterested party. And since Gilbert was Stratford's friend, even his word could be called into question. He had to expose Lunenburg in such a way that they would believe him without question. But how?

"What do you think we should do, Gilbert?"

"I have been wondering the same."

"The first person who has a right to know is the real Baron Hans von Lunenburg. Is it not our duty to tell him?"

"Yes. We should have thought of that before we left London, I suppose." Gilbert let out a resigned sigh.

"I was too much in a hurry to let my friends know and to see Dorothea again. I have missed her. More than I ever thought possible." He pictured light ringlets falling on each side of her softly curved cheeks. He remembered the sound of her voice and the tone of her sweet laughter. He couldn't wait to see her face once more.

"There will be plenty of time to visit Lady Dorothea. First, the business at hand must be settled."

"I suppose we should send a letter by post," Stratford suggested. "But even with good information at hand, I feel most reluctant to send a missive to a man I do not even know to tell him that someone here is impersonating him. Why should he even believe me?"

"Why should he not? You have no sinister motive for making such a suggestion."

"Still. . ." He snapped his fingers. "You say you are acquainted with him."

"Through a distant family connection. I cannot say I know him as an intimate."

"Still, why not invite him to visit you here at my estate? We can lure him here by offering to have his portrait painted by a promising new artist."

Gilbert considered the suggestion. "It is worth a try."

As soon as they arrived home, Stratford didn't delay in entering his study where he sat at his mahogany secretary and wrote the missive to be sent to London. As he sealed the letter, he allowed himself a triumphant sigh. At last, he was on his way to ridding himself of Baron Hans von Lunenburg—also known as Clayton Forsythe—forever.

❦

A few days later as Stratford scooped up the last of his poached eggs, the butler entered the dining room. "You have a letter, milord."

Stratford took the epistle. "Thank you. That will be all."

"Yes, sir."

Gilbert, sitting at the other end of the table, sent him a quizzical look. "Could this be the one we have been hoping to receive?"

"I think so." Stratford rushed to open it and looked at the signature. "Yes, it is!" He hurried to read the reply from London written in an unfamiliar scrawl. As soon as he scanned the message, Stratford saw his hope dissolve into nothingness. He threw the heavy cream-colored sheet of paper onto the mahogany dining table with a firm *whoosh*.

"What is that all about?" Gilbert asked.

"See for yourself." He picked up the offending epistle and handed it to his friend, who read it aloud:

Dear Lord Brunswick,
  I would like to thank you and Gilbert Meara, Esq., for your gracious invitation to join you for hunting and fishing at your country estate and for the opportunity to commission my portrait with a promising new artist. Regrettably,

business here prohibits me from making the journey at present, so I must decline.

I do hope the opportunity will arise for the two of us to become acquainted at another pleasant occasion. Please send my kindest regards to Gilbert.

Yours,
Hans, Baron von Lunenburg

Gilbert tapped the letter on the table and laid it on top of the smooth polished wood. "I am so sorry our plan failed, but I would not let discouragement overtake me if I were you. Clayton Forsythe seems to be having a grand time amid his new friends out here in the country. And until they all run out of money, I venture he will be more than happy to enjoy their fine food and hospitality during his stay here."

"Until they all run out of money indeed." Stratford remembered Dorothea and how she hovered near Helen's door that first night he spied her. How afraid she looked with no money and nowhere to turn for help but to a distant relative. Having to accept the kindness of a stranger must have been quite a blow. He was only grateful he had encouraged her to pursue her talent so she would not be forced to take on a reduced station.

The thought of Clayton Forsythe taking advantage of his friends, perhaps putting them in similar peril, made him shudder. Yet if he didn't make the right move at the proper time to expose him, all would be lost. Gilbert was right; Forsythe was in no hurry to leave. Exposure could happen later. And Stratford would make sure it did.

nine

"You have been quiet all day. Are you not excited about the party?" Dorothea asked Helen as the carriage made its way over country lanes to the event.

"I suppose." Helen looked absently out of the window.

"I have been admiring the Wickford estate ever since I saw it when we passed it the first night I arrived here. Such a beautiful old home, sitting so proudly on top of the hill. How magnificent the house must appear inside!"

"That monstrosity?" Helen scrunched her nose.

"My, but you seem to be in a sour mood today, Helen. I have never heard you make such an observation about any of the other estates."

"I am so sorry. I am not myself. My stomach has been feeling odd all day."

Luke leaned over and took both of her hands in his. "Are you sure you feel quite all right, my dear? We really do not have to attend if you are not up to the task."

"Oh, yes we do. I responded last week for all of us, and I would never want to inconvenience Lady Lydia with an uneven number of guests at her dinner table. You know as well as I that such a faux pas would be quite rude and possibly cause us never to be invited to another social event for years to come."

"But if you are ill. . ."

"That is quite all right. I shall sip on tea, and that will soothe my stomach." Helen clutched her abdomen as the carriage hit a bump. She recovered and turned her face to Dorothea. "You should enjoy this party. Even though Lady Lydia is a dreadful bore, she usually invites interesting guests. I understand she has visitors from Dover who have just been abroad."

"How exciting. They should be intriguing."

But Stratford will be even more intriguing.

When Dorothea and her party entered the large hall of the Wickford manor house, she took in a breath. The Wickford coat of arms greeted the guests, an impressive display indeed. Burgundy velvet draperies adorned each window, and the Chippendale-style furnishings looked to be as costly as those she had seen in London's finest homes. The wallpaper showed a bucolic scene, the figures outlined in burgundy against cream. Expensive curiosities that appeared to have been collected from travels to exotic places decorated tables, walls, and shelves. Not a speck of dust was to be seen. Everything gleamed.

Dorothea hadn't thought such a feat was possible, but inspection of the banquet tables demonstrated that Lady Lydia managed to serve even more varieties of food than Helen had offered at Hans's birthday party. The treats emanated scents as pleasing to the nose as their appearance presented a feast for the eyes. The offerings had been positioned on the table in such a way that the colors blended well. Varieties of pastries were emphasized by creative decorations of various colors of icing—red flavored with cherry juice and orange with marmalade. Still, the stuffed oysters wrapped in bacon strips and covered in white cream were her finest delicacy and the topic of every conversation that focused on food.

"Delicious, is it not?" Dorothea asked Helen as she bit into a cheese turnover.

"Yes, I suppose so."

Helen's agreement seemed halfhearted, and Dorothea knew Helen well enough by that time to realize that her cousin's stomach wasn't the source of her distress. Dorothea suspected she seethed at the idea of the variety and bounty of her buffet being thought of as less grand than Lady Lydia's. She decided to find someone else with whom to converse before Helen's ire could be stirred into a frenzy.

Soon Dorothea spotted Stratford. As it always did, her

heart beat with joy when she drank in his appearance. She desperately wanted to draw closer to him so they could speak together, but she knew that to make her way over to him would appear much too bold even though their fondness for one another was known among their friends. Helen was always chastising Dorothea about presenting to the world the ideal image of womanhood: obedience and subservience to men, meekness, reticence, and a still and quiet beauty. She wasn't certain as to the degree of her success in any of these factors, but for her cousin's sake, and for the sake of her dear mother's memory, she tried.

She made herself content to speak with the other women. By now, she felt more comfortable in her ability to recall their names at short notice and could remember enough details about their lives to make intelligent queries for updates. All in all, she really was feeling more like the social butterfly Helen had earlier described her to be.

Finally, near the conclusion of the party, Stratford came up beside her. The clean smell of citrus emanated from him in a subtle and pleasing manner. "This has been a lovely party, has it not?"

"Indeed." She waved her fan.

"I am in need of fresh air. Would you care to take a walk in the garden?"

Dorothea waved her fan. "Yes, I would enjoy the opportunity for fresh air. And I am eager to see the formal gardens. I understand they are magnificent."

"Yes, especially since the first flowers of the season have already bloomed. No doubt Lady Lydia has made certain there are plenty of torches burning to allow us to see her garden as well as it can be seen in the dark."

"Based on the exquisite attention to detail that I have witnessed so far at the Wickford house, I suggest you are right indeed."

"Then let us see for ourselves." He took her by the elbow and escorted her out of doors in a discreet manner. They walked through the garden, ignoring a few other couples who had also taken refuge from the crowd. The more they progressed, the more distant the sound of the voices and music of the party sounded. Though she had enjoyed the activity, Dorothea found that at present she welcomed the comparative silence.

"So, does the foliage measure up to your expectations?" Stratford asked her.

She studied the immaculate pathway of crushed stones defined by a tall, sculpted boxwood hedge. Flowering shrubs were strategically placed to add just the right amount of color among the green. The night air mingled with the gentle scent of the flora around them and smelled fresh with promise. Dorothea noticed larger-than-life statues of various gods and goddesses of mythology, each lit by a flaming torch. She couldn't understand the love of false idols that spurred the rich to include their likenesses in their gardens, but she was not their judge. She only knew that her parents never adorned their gardens with such, and neither would she.

She decided to take a safe conversational path. "Like everything else I have seen here tonight, the gardens exceed my expectations. The Wickfords have put on a spectacle to be spoken of long after the last guest has departed this evening."

"Yes, I would agree that they spared very little expense. And they have created a pleasant place of solitude, indeed. But this garden did not bloom with a single orchid until your appearance here tonight."

Dorothea stared at the pathway ahead, the compliment making her feel shy.

They approached a bench. "Would you care to take a seat?" Stratford offered.

"Yes." She nodded and seated herself. At first the bench felt chilly, but the warmth of their bodies soon brought it to a level of comfort.

He sat beside her. "I am halfway surprised Lunenburg has

not chased us out here in a jealous rage by now."

Lunenburg. She would have been just as happy not to hear his name. He had pursued her more than once over the course of the evening, but she had managed to avoid all but the most superficial conversation with him.

She managed a chuckle. "I think he knows by now that my interest in him is limited to how he will appear in his portrait."

"Are you sure?"

"Oh, he has tried—" She stopped herself. "I beg your pardon. I should never have said anything so vain."

"I would not consider your statement vain if it indeed reflects the truth. And I do believe it does."

"It does." Dorothea looked at a nearby corner and noticed a statue of Venus.

Stratford followed her gaze. "The mythical goddess of love."

She studied the statue of the robe-clad ancient beauty. "Apparently Lady Lydia is quite the romantic. Or perhaps her husband is."

"And you? Are you fond of romantic notions?"

She felt a smile kiss her lips. "I have been accused of having my head in the clouds. All that reading of silly love stories, you know."

"You have mentioned that. I find your hobby quite charming." He looked to the moon that broke through a clouded sky. "Just past a new moon."

Dorothea looked upward to see the thinnest of thin crescents in the sky. "Yes. How pretty."

"I will let you in on a secret. Despite all the fuss made over a full moon, I think a crescent moon is equally romantic."

She looked into his face. "As do I. Perhaps because it offers such an intriguing shape—and less light." Then, realizing she had made a comment that could be construed as a flirtation, she returned her attention to the moon.

"All the better for stolen kisses?" he whispered in her ear.

His warm breath against her skin sent her whirling into yet another fantasyland. She wondered if he would take the opportunity to illustrate his observation. Her heart beat with longing, and she knew many women would allow their beaux to kiss them whether the moon was full or new, but she was not one of those women. She hesitated, not wanting to resist but knowing that she must.

He glanced her way. His expression told her that his own yearning matched—or even exceeded—her own. He hesitated, then seemed to think better of it. He turned his face to the moon.

Initial disappointment was soon overcome by relief. He had just proven beyond a doubt that he was a gentleman, one who was willing to wait for physical longings to be expressed. She realized at that moment that she had tempted him by agreeing to walk alone with him in the gardens, even though others were milling around, as well. And then she had had the nerve not to turn away her face when he mentioned a kiss.

Father, forgive me. Tempting the man I love was not my purpose.

"We must go back inside," she said, determined to put her prayer into quick action.

"Are you cold?"

She rose from her spot on the bench. "No. No indeed. It is just that—"

He stood beside her. "You love me. And you know I am tempted by you."

"I—I—"

He took her in a gentle way by the forearms and peered into her eyes. "I do not mind saying it. I love you. I have loved you since that first moment I saw you hovering in the Syms's foyer, looking quite afraid and anxious."

"So you felt sorry for me?"

"No. I was too busy wondering how I could learn who you were to feel any pity. After all, you were wearing a fine traveling suit. You did not appear to be in any want—

although I could envision you being the envy of every other woman in the parish."

"If I am envied by anyone, it is because I am privileged to spend time with the most sought-after man from here to London." Though her remark could have been construed as coy, she meant what she said.

"Do you mean Lunenburg?"

She let out an impatient noise. "You love to exasperate me, do you not?"

"Perhaps I am afraid that if I do not vex you, I might do something more dangerous."

"Then I had best keep the topic on the other man." She tapped him on the shoulder with the tip of her fan. "Perhaps to eager investors and to a few silly women he appears to be desirable. And I suppose if I were to be fair in my assessment, I would have to admit he does possess a few good qualities— a knack for telling a story, a degree of charm—"

Stratford cleared his throat. His dark eyebrows rose in a mocking way.

She gave him a crooked smile. "But you possess all those things in even more abundance."

"You flatter me."

"Do I? Maybe I am blinded by love." Her tone fell to softness.

"If you are, I pray you will remain blind to my faults all the days of your life."

"And may you be just as unenlightened as to mine."

He took her chin in his hand. She looked deeply into his eyes that glistened in the moonlight. "My dear, you are flawless."

A familiar voice interrupted. "There you are, Brunswick!"

The sudden intrusion made Dorothea startle.

Stratford also gave a little jump. He turned and glared at the figure approaching them through the shadows. "Lunenburg."

The name brought Dorothea down from the soft pedestal

on which Stratford had just set her. Her spirit descended back to the cold, hard ground. The disruption of their interlude made her realize that her stomach had felt as though it were flitting in circles, and her head suffered a degree of lightness. If flying without wings were possible, Dorothea could have picked herself up and journeyed through the sky, up to the moon—until her feet hit the cold ground. She looked at Hans, but her mental focus remained on Stratford.

"Do come back out of this chill," Hans implored. "The games are commencing in the drawing room."

"Games. Yes." Stratford's voice fell flat.

Dorothea noticed that the others who had been nearby in the garden were returning to the house. She and Stratford had no choice. Considering she had been an instant away from kissing Stratford, perhaps the interruption had been for the best.

"Oh, how fun!" She surprised herself by the degree of enthusiasm she managed, as if Hans hadn't interrupted the most intriguing, fascinating, thrilling, exhilarating, astounding, lovely conversation of her life. She tugged on Stratford's sleeve. "Do let us go."

Hans sent Stratford a triumphant smile that suggested that he was pleased with his timing. She wished he would go on ahead of them so at least she could enjoy walking arm in arm with Stratford for a moment, but he kept pace with them, chattering and gossiping all the while. Dorothea didn't offer any enchanting observations in return. She noticed Stratford remained reticent, as well.

As the next hour evaporated into eternity during heated contests, Dorothea claimed not a victory that night. Stratford seemed to be off his game, as well. She didn't wonder as to why he seemed distracted.

❧

Stratford tried not to sulk as he lost game after game. Lunenburg was in fine form and relished every victory. Stratford felt certain Lunenburg's greatest success was spurred by the triumph of interrupting his conversation with Dorothea. Stratford had been so close to kissing her lips—lips he had dreamed about ever since the night he first saw her.

Maybe the Lord had used Lunenburg to keep him from acting less than a gentleman to the woman he loved. After all, he had not proposed marriage. At least not yet.

He couldn't concentrate well on charades, for his mind was elsewhere. On the beautiful vision sitting near him. Dorothea.

Heavenly Father, I thank Thee in all humility that she really does love me—and not because of a sense of gratitude. And I thank Thee for letting her heart not belong to Lunenburg. Thou art aware, Lord, that I would never want any woman who harbored feelings of love for another man. I thank Thee for Thy mercy.

Yet as he made halfhearted guesses in response to the frantic motions of his teammates, Stratford felt a tugging at his heart. He fought the tugging, but as soon as he did, his conscience pulled the mental rope with more vigor than he could stand. Like it or not, he had been sent a revelation. He had to tell Dorothea the truth.

As soon as he could gracefully break away from the games, Stratford made his way across the room to her. A thinning crowd made his movements more obvious than they had been earlier in the evening. Still, he had to tell her. He had to catch her before Luke summoned his family to depart the festivities.

Dorothea must have been watching him, for she didn't hesitate to turn his way and make her excuses to the women as soon as he stood by her side.

"I must tell you something before I leave the party," he whispered.

She surveyed the room. "But the people. Someone will overhear."

"Then let us escape to the garden."

She hesitated. "Should we risk going back outdoors?"

"Do not be afraid. I will not allow my lips to venture anywhere near yours."

Even though I want nothing more.

She blushed a most becoming shade of pink. "But surely someone will notice. People will talk."

"Then let them if they are that jealous of us. I shall not keep you long."

She sent him a tempting smile, one whose promise he wished he could fulfill. Instead, once they were in the garden, he made sure to remain near the light. Surely being in the open would help him keep his word that there would be no display of his yearning for her.

She seemed to understand his meaning. "Whatever you have to tell me must be important."

"It is." He kept his voice brisk on purpose.

She clutched his forearm. "Whatever you have done or have not done, whatever secret you hold to your past, does not matter to me now. And it never will."

"So you think I am some sort of criminal?" He chuckled in spite of himself.

"Intriguing, yes. A criminal, no." Relief filled her voice all the same.

He took her hands in his. Her soft fingers had absorbed some of the chill. He was glad he had made a gesture that would warm them. "What I have to tell you is not criminal, although I confess I have been keeping a secret from you, one that I wish to reveal before we carry on any further than we have on this night."

"Oh." Her mouth dropped open in the slight manner of one who was surprised.

"The secret concerns you."

"Me?"

"Yes." He hesitated. How could he tell her? What words would be right? He searched his mind, but nothing sounded precise. Not the way he wanted it to sound. How could he tell her that he had been deceiving her all this time? Yet he had to let her know. The Holy Spirit would not want it to be any other way. He sent up a silent prayer for help.

"Go on," she prodded. "You can tell me anything."

"All right. I shall." He took in a breath, held both of her hands even more tightly, and hoped that her fingers that had grown warm within his grasp would fortify him. He looked down at her hands, so soft and trusting, enveloped in his stronger ones. He wanted to shield her from all harm. Yes, that was it. "Ever since I saw you that first night, I have wanted to protect you."

"From what?"

"From the world. From Baron von Lunenburg in particular." Knowing that Lunenburg was really Clayton Forsythe, Stratford prided himself on his ability not to trip over his assumed name.

Her grip on his hands loosened, though she didn't let go. "From Hans? Why would you want to protect me from him? It is no mystery that the two of you are not the best of friends, but I have told you all about how he called in a favor with a judge so that the huge gambling debts I inherited from Father would be forgiven."

"Yes, you told me your story."

"Then you will understand why I will never forget how he helped me when I needed someone most—when no one else, not even Helen, would or could."

"He came to your assistance, yes. But for a price."

"No. That is not true." Her eyes took on a pleading light.

So she persisted in her innocence. He wanted nothing more than to tell her about how Lunenburg had boasted to him that his favor had just bought himself a mistress— Dorothea. Yet when he looked into her eyes, he could see the hurt that already plagued her soul, and he couldn't tell her about Hans's sordid plans. Even if he did, he sensed she might not believe him. And no one—not Luke and certainly not Lunenburg—would be willing to confirm his story.

Stratford struggled to find the right words. "Dorothea."

He squeezed her hands. "Your bills were settled but not in the manner you thought."

"He. . .he did not keep his word? He did not write to the judge?"

"I am sure he would have kept his word to you," Stratford forced himself to admit. "But he did not have to call in his favor after all. I am the one who paid your father's debts."

She let go of his hands. "You—you what?"

"I paid them."

"You? You paid those awful men who robbed my father?" She took a step back away from him.

Stratford tried to contain his shock. His confession wasn't going well at all. Instead of being filled with a sense of thankfulness, she seemed furious with him. Now he wished for the gratitude he had once so feared!

"I cannot say I condone gambling or that I harbor a great degree of sympathy or compassion for the proprietors of gaming establishments. But as Christians, can we justify not paying our debts?"

"Of course we should pay our debts. If they are honest ones."

"I understand what you are trying to say," he hastened to admit. "Believe me, Dorothea, I have struggled with this. Words are inadequate to explain how much and how long this has troubled me. But in fact, there are no provisions or exceptions in the Bible regarding whatever we owe. As far as I can see, all debts are to be paid in full."

She looked at the flat stone in front of her feet.

Taking compassion upon what had to be her embarrass-ment, Stratford sought to comfort her. "During my struggle, I found comfort in a certain passage and put it to memory. Jesus told us in the Gospel of St. Matthew, 'But I say unto you, Love your enemies, bless them that curse you, do good to them that hate you, and pray for them which despitefully use you, and persecute you; that ye may be the children of your Father which is in heaven: for he maketh his sun to rise on the evil and on the good, and sendeth rain on the just and on the unjust.'"

"I congratulate you on your excellent memorization and perhaps even application of that particular passage of scripture." Her tone held anything but praise. "But St. Matthew also wrote that Jesus said that we should love our neighbor as ourselves. And if you had taken that scripture to heart, you would have shown me enough Christian love to trust me with such vital information about my own life."

"I battled with that, truly I did. But I never wanted you to love me out of gratitude alone. Such an emotion can easily be confused with love."

"Especially by a weak-minded woman such as myself?" Her voice registered not anger but hurt.

Mortification at her response struck his heart. "I would never say such. I cannot believe you could harbor such a notion after all the conversations we have shared over these past months."

"You are so high-minded that you cannot even bring yourself to think of me as a weak-minded woman?"

"No. No, I tell you."

"So you say. But based on your actions, I find your protests hard to swallow. Can you really believe that I am so feeble in both mind and will that I would accept a suitor on the basis of gratitude alone?"

"No. I do not."

"If only I could believe you. Good evening, Lord Brunswick." She turned and started to walk back toward the house.

He picked up his steps to join her. "But that is not the entire story. I have much more to say. If only you will listen—"

She failed to turn but rather increased her pace. "Good evening, Lord Brunswick."

"Please, I—"

His entreaties fell on her back. He stopped himself as he saw that chasing her was of no use. Stratford had paid a dear price indeed for his confession. He had lost her forever.

ten

As he went home that evening, Stratford could hardly believe the turn of events. How could the happiest night of his life so suddenly turn into the bitterest? How could one confession take Dorothea so near a kiss to fleeing in the opposite direction?

Cringing as he recalled the dispute, Stratford wondered how he would ever see her on friendly terms again. He remembered the hurt and disappointment he saw on her face. He remembered how she had spun on her heel and flown back into the house. He had searched the thin crowd for her, but she had disappeared. No doubt she had convinced Helen and Luke to take her home without delay. How much of his confession had she revealed to them? Did they think him a fool—or worse?

What did it matter? He didn't care what anyone thought of him except for Dorothea. Granted, fear of her continued ire had discouraged him from making an assertive effort to regain her favor. He took comfort in the fact that she had spoken no more than a few courtesies to anyone present.

If only she had sought him out! But she had not.

For the first time in his life, he knew the pain of a broken heart.

He decided to give Dorothea some time before trying to pursue her again. Perhaps Helen could convince her to give him another chance. No matter what Dorothea said, he was determined to make amends. Perhaps God's will was for them to be apart—but if so, he prayed that their separation would prove to be God's will for only a short while.

Stratford felt one certainty in his heart. He wasn't about to give up his love for Dorothea without a fight. And he knew the best strategy for regaining her confidence.

After the weekend was through, he wrote her a missive:

My dearest Dorothea,

I pray that this message finds you well and in a humor to grant me a favor I do not deserve. That favor is your forgiveness. I regret anything I said or did that caused you the least bit of heartache, trouble, embarrassment, or offense. How can I make amends to you, my dearest? I can think of nothing too unreasonable, too difficult, or too impossible for me to try if it would help you love me again.

Please respond as soon as you can. After I receive your answer, I will ride like the wind to be by your side if only for the briefest of moments. If only I can hear your sweet voice that no music can duplicate, see your face that the word "beautiful" is insufficient to describe, touch your hands to which no velvet can compare in softness. Then, and only then, can I claim any amount of happiness once again.

Please send me a favorable reply. I await your letter eagerly.

Yours,
Stratford

He folded the paper and heated a pot of crimson sealing wax over a candle's flame. With care he dripped the hot resin on the fold to close the letter, then stamped it with the seal of his family coat of arms. He blew a kiss onto the wax, schoolboyish action though it was. Perhaps now that she had had a few days to reconsider their conversation, she would give him a favorable response.

He waited a day. And another day.

Nothing.

At least she hadn't returned his letter back to him with a message never to try to contact her again. But that fact comforted him little.

He tried sending a letter to her each day. Perhaps if he

persisted in sending his messengers to the estate, someone would notice and he would be invited to visit, if not by Dorothea, perhaps by Luke. Then he could hope that they could bump into one another. Perhaps if she saw him again, the situation might take a turn for the better.

Hope persisting in his heart, Stratford sent Dorothea a letter each day, five days in a row.

Still no response.

His foul mood evidenced itself at breakfast on Friday.

"So your lady friend still has not sent you an answer?" Gilbert guessed.

Stratford cut into the slice of bacon on the china plate painted with pink flowers, a feminine pattern selected by his mother when his parents were first betrothed. "No. I have no idea why. I wish she would write something, anything. Even if she were to tell me she never wanted to see me again, I would think she would grant me the courtesy of a response."

"Perhaps she thinks if she ignores you, you will give up your quest for her."

"She knows me better than that."

Gilbert set down a glass he had just drained of juice. "Fine. Sulk all you like, but she cannot see you in your misery, so what good does a sour humor do for anyone? I suggest you ride into the village and take lunch in the tavern. Maybe seeing some other people will cheer you."

Stratford considered the idea. "I must admit, the thought does sound like a good idea. Will you not join me?"

"Not this time. I have some correspondence I must complete before I can consider any sort of outing. You have been keeping me so busy with your excellent opportunities for fishing that I fear I have fallen quite behind."

"I am so glad I have been able to provide you with the entertainment you prefer, my friend. Do remember me in your correspondence to our mutual acquaintances, will you not?"

"Indeed."

That afternoon Stratford decided to take his friend's advice, and so he rode into the village. Perhaps the acquisition of a stylish new garment would lift his spirits. As he hitched his horse to a vacant post near the hub of the commercial center, he spotted the only man he didn't want to see. Clayton Forsythe. Just seeing the man left Stratford with a queasy feeling. If only he had told Dorothea the cheat's real identity first rather than just revealing that he himself, not the imposter, had paid her bills. But Dorothea had abandoned their conversation—and him—before anything else could be revealed. As far as Dorothea knew, Forsythe was still Baron Hans von Lunenburg. And Stratford knew that Clayton Forsythe wanted to keep it that way.

"Brunswick!" the man called before Stratford could pretend he hadn't seen him. Lunenburg crossed the dirt path that served as the main thoroughfare to speak to him. "It is good to see you again, old man. Was that not an excellent gathering at the Wickfords' the other night?"

"Excellent." He petted his horse on the nose, not wanting to ask the question that formed on his lips. He found to his distress that he couldn't stop himself. "How is your portrait coming along?"

"Excellent. You may not know much, old man, but you do know art. She is painting a most exquisite portrait of my personage. The definitive image of my lifetime, I will venture."

"Good." His voice managed to express a deceptive amount of vigor.

"I would almost say I owe you a debt. In fact, perhaps I do. I have asked permission to court Dorothea, and Luke has been gracious enough to grant that permission."

Stratford froze. "Indeed." He felt his lips barely move. "And the lady has accepted?"

Lunenburg guffawed with skilled overconfidence. "Considering that everyone witnessed your harsh exchange at the party, how can you even bring her acceptance into question?"

Of course! How could he have expected not a soul to be privy to Dorothea's hurried flight from him? Could he have thought that no one would have observed the way he chased her, begging her to reconsider? And naturally, such a small parish would relish spreading such intriguing gossip.

Stratford tried to control his breathing from becoming ragged with rage. Sending up a silent prayer for the discipline not to give in to his anger, he reached into his satchel for a cube of sugar and fed it to the horse. He watched the animal consume the treat so he wouldn't have to look Lunenburg in the eye.

"Your silence only confirms how right I am," Lunenburg said. "Lady Dorothea Witherspoon is no longer your concern."

Fuming, Stratford decided not to retort, lest he regret his words. The horse finished his treat, and Stratford tipped his hat. "I have many errands to run here in the village, and the merchants will be closing their doors in an hour. I must be on my way. Good afternoon."

"Good afternoon." A triumphant smile curved Lunenburg's lips.

Stratford knitted his brow as a dark mood overtook him. Unwanted images of Dorothea holding court with Clayton Forsythe sickened him.

A sore loser, are you not?

Stratford put his nagging conscience aside. Perhaps he deserved such self-recrimination. Perhaps his confession had only heightened her opinion of Lunenburg. And that was the danger. Even if he deserved Dorothea's spurning, he knew one thing: Dorothea did not deserve to be taken into the web of a confidence man—an insect who wrapped innocent victims in a silken thread of sweet lies and cunning deceit. Stratford imagined that if Dorothea continued her ill-advised dalliance, she would discover the man would strip her of all she held dear—her pride, what remained of her fortune, her very future. No. He couldn't allow it.

Even if she doesn't want me, surely she must be saved from Clayton.

Surely a plan would come to mind without delay. He could only hope.

❧

Helen walked out the west portico, looking for her cousin. "Oh, Dorothea, Luke just told me! How fortunate you are that Baron von Lunenburg has finally asked to court you!" Helen nearly jumped up and down in her glee.

Sitting in a rocker so she could take advantage of the sun even though the ball of fire played hide-and-seek amid clouds, Dorothea looked up from her book. After her devotional and Bible reading, she had selected a silly story in hopes of taking her mind off of her argument with Stratford and her nagging questions as to why he hadn't bothered to try to contact her since the night of the party—the night that took her to the heights of a mountaintop, then sent her crashing down to the rocks at its bottom. Dorothea was only too happy to immerse herself in the sorrows of a heroine who had just lost her only true love to a kidnapping by a gang of pirates. But Helen, well-intentioned though she was, had only brought Dorothea back to a cheerless reality.

"Yes. He did ask." Her voice reflected as much dread as an ill-prepared student would display when presented with a surprise test.

Helen sat in the rocker beside Dorothea's and placed her hand on her arm. "What is the matter, Dorothea?"

How could she tell Helen? "I—I have not made up my mind whether or not I want to be courted by Hans. Or anyone else."

"Surely you jest. Any other woman in the parish would be thrilled for the chance. How many times have I told you that Baron von Lunenburg is a wealthy and popular man?"

She ran her fingertips over the edge of the pages of her novel. "He must not be too popular, since I seem to be the only woman he visits."

"On the contrary, the fact that he visits here every day is only serving to make you—and us—more popular. Everyone wins."

Everyone but me.

Hans was charming enough, but how could Dorothea tell Helen that she just didn't love him? Not like she loved Stratford. Even though they had argued, they had been apart no more than an hour before Dorothea saw that her feelings of adoration for Stratford remained. She thought of him constantly whether she wanted to or not.

She sensed Hans must have somehow discovered that she and Stratford had quarreled. Why else would he be so persistent in his pursuit of her? Then again, everyone in the parish gossiped about his love of competition. Dorothea wondered whether Hans really was interested in her or if beating out Stratford added excitement to the game. Whatever his motivation, as Helen pointed out, he was relentless about taking every opportunity to visit her. Dorothea was human enough to find the attention of a popular and attractive man flattering, but she couldn't love Hans.

Whenever Hans visited, Dorothea was polite but cool. How could she have any regard for a man who would let her think he did her a great favor when in fact someone else did? Why did Stratford pay her bills rather than letting Hans call in a favor with the judge? Did he feel sorry for her? Even worse, was he trying to buy her attentions? But if he was, then why did he wait to tell her about the arrangement after she had already confessed her love?

Heavenly Father, please let the answers to all of my questions soon become evident.

Dorothea wanted to counter Helen's assumption that she should encourage Hans. Yet she had little ammunition to contradict her cousin's opinion. Since the evening she and Stratford had argued, he hadn't tried to contact her. Despite her harsh words, she longed to hear from him. Even if he would stop by just to see Luke, she could contrive to see him. But she never saw him, and no missive or message of any sort arrived. If only she had taken longer to complete his portrait. Her only current commissions were of Hans and of a neighbor's daughter.

Did her outburst extinguish Stratford's love for her? She sighed. If their love was so weak, it could never withstand long years of marriage. Perhaps the dispute was God's way of protecting her from future heartbreak. If only her heart didn't have to break now!

eleven

A fortnight had passed without a word from Stratford. Dorothea waited and watched, but no message arrived. Once she even thought she saw a messenger from the Brunswick estate ride up the drive, missive in hand. But Helen had assured her that no message had been sent to her.

So when she peered out the window and saw Stratford himself arriving on horseback just as if it were another day of a portrait sitting, she gasped aloud. Seeing the dashing figure, she could hardly contain her feelings.

If only he could be mine! What a fool I was to send him away!

Still, she was tempted to run to her room. When she last saw him, he was begging for her to give him a chance, to listen to his side of the story. Perhaps he had changed his mind and decided that he had every right to be angry with her. Maybe the purpose of his visit was to unleash his ire, to tell her what he really thought of her. What if his rage had grown to such an extent that he planned to advise Luke to tell her that he was no longer willing to extend his hospitality to her? Perhaps such actions were the least that she deserved.

Or what if he planned to apologize? What if he wanted to throw himself at her feet, to beg her forgiveness?

Or what if she had overreacted and she was the one who owed him an apology?

Whatever his intention, she had to face him sooner or later.

Heavenly Father, give me strength, and guide my words and actions.

She decided to remain in the drawing room, standing erect to show a confidence she didn't feel.

When his feet hit the front steps, Dorothea rushed to the

door. If the butler answered and Stratford didn't ask to see her, her opportunity would be lost. Perhaps she was wrong to race the faithful servant to the door. Stratford was sure to know it was unusual for Dorothea to answer his knock. Would he be able to discern her plan?

So what if he does?

"Dorothea!" Then, seeming to remember his manners, he tipped his hat.

"Stratford. Do come in." She stepped aside and allowed him to enter. As he walked by her, she noticed the familiar scent he wore—a clean fragrance of citrus.

"Should I tell Luke you are here?"

"In due time, I suppose." He searched the foyer, apparently looking for someone to dispense with his coat and hat. She took both without a word and hung them on the rack near the entrance, realizing she needed to search for some type of explanation as to why she herself had answered the door. "I. . .uh. . .the butler is in the back of the house, and I saw no need to ring for him to answer when I just happened to be looking out and spotted you arriving." There. She had managed to tell the truth.

"I would rather see you than he any day. Or anyone else in this house, for that matter."

"Really?" So he wasn't still vexed with her after all!

"Really, if I may be so bold." Query lit upon his eyes—fear that he had offended her?

"And if I may be so bold, I do not regret your sentiment."

The look in his eyes told her he had missed her as much as she had longed for him.

"Dorothea." He took her in his embrace and stroked her cheek.

"I thought you were angry with me."

"And I thought you were angry with me."

"I was for a time." Realizing she couldn't—or shouldn't—remain in his arms indefinitely despite her aching desire to do so, she broke free of his embrace, though gently. "But

I am angry no longer. After I had time to reflect upon our discourse, I came to the realization that I should not be cross with a man who was willing to make such a grand gesture to me, a stranger he had just met. I still do not understand why you chose to pay off my debts instead of letting Hans call in his favor with his friend the judge."

"I—I do not know that I should tell you."

"Have I not a right to know?"

"The reason, I am afraid, is quite indelicate." He peered into the drawing room. "Might we go somewhere more comfortable—and private?"

Her curiosity was piqued to the point that she was unable to resist his suggestion. She escorted him into the room and took a seat. He sat across from her, with the tea table positioned between them.

She didn't waste time urging him to get to the point. "So what you have to say is indelicate?"

He cleared his throat. "Obviously you are still unaware of the price you would have paid had I let you accept such a large favor from that man."

Dorothea felt confused. "What price? Please, tell me what you mean. I must know."

"I have struggled for a long time in seeking the best words to convey an indelicate subject. How shall I say this without offending your sensitive ears?" He sighed, and when he did, a look that told her he felt the weight of the world upon himself crossed his countenance.

"I shall be strong."

"Very well. I spoke to him soon after he saw you that first night. He boasted to me that he expected a sort of payment from you that no woman of your substance and character should be expected to render."

Dorothea thought for a moment, then realized what Stratford meant. "Oh, no. Surely you do not mean it." In an effort to remain calm, she leaned her back against the chair and fanned herself. "Could you have mistaken his intent?"

"I am afraid I did not mistake his intent. I would give anything not to be forced into such an admission, but he shared his intent with me in no uncertain terms. He was quite proud of himself, really. And I knew why. You are the most beautiful woman in the parish."

"You are too kind. I can think of many women here who are much more beautiful than I."

"Not to my eyes."

She set her fan in her lap but continued to clutch it with her fingertips. "So that is why you decided to rescue me? Because you fancy me beautiful?"

"I admit that did not discourage me. But after we met and conversed, I could see plainly that you had no idea what his plans were for you. I could not allow him to have his way. He is a cad. His manners offend me."

"I do not see how you could stop him, although you obviously succeeded. And for that, I owe you an eternal debt of gratitude."

"Which is exactly why I did not want to tell you what I had done. I did not want you to look upon me as some sort of knight in shining armor but as a man of flesh and blood. And I did not want you to feel that you owed me your consideration only because I paid your debt. If so, I would have simply replaced the baron."

"If not gratitude, then what did you want?"

"Lunenburg asked me the same thing when I made the offer, and I will repeat to you what I said to him. Believe it or not, I wanted nothing but to show compassion to a woman who was obviously a fellow Christian."

"Hmm. Then you chose the role of Good Samaritan." Her voice was colored by disappointment.

He contemplated her response. "You have a point. I did not think of that story at the time, but I can see why you make the connection. In all frankness, I felt led by my desire to obey the Savior to pay your debt and to keep you from falling into the clutches of an unscrupulous man."

She considered his actions and the consequences she would have faced had he chosen to ignore her plight. "Then I really do owe you a debt of gratitude."

"No, I told you. You owe me nothing. And even if you tried to repay me with money, time, or in some other way, I would not accept any offering."

"You have more than my friendship. I think you know that."

"Do I? I thought I had lost you."

"And I, you," she admitted.

"Why? Just because we exchanged a few regrettable words in the heat of emotion?"

"That and the fact that you never tried to contact me. Not once." She set her gaze upon the empty tea table in hopes he wouldn't witness the hurt she knew would reveal itself upon her countenance.

"I beg your pardon. After three days had passed with no word from you, I realized I had to make a gesture of regret. I wrote you a letter every day." His voice took a slight rise in pitch, the sign of an exasperated man.

Dorothea's questions and vexation soon rose to the same level as his. "Indeed? But that is not possible. I never received any missives from you."

"None?"

"Not the first one."

He leaned toward her. "But I gave them to my most reliable servant. He has never let me down before."

Dorothea tried to discern what could have happened. She could see from his mannerisms and obvious shock that Stratford told the truth. Indeed, she had no reason to believe he had ever lied to her in the past. Something must have happened to keep her from receiving his correspondence.

"Did he tell you he delivered the letters directly into my hands?" she asked.

Stratford paused to consider her question. "No."

"Tell me something. Did you send your messenger here

Thursday morning just before the noon hour?"

"Yes."

"The butler told me the message was for Luke. He bore false witness on someone's orders, no doubt." Anger followed on the heels of disappointment for Dorothea. "I wonder who did receive the letters, then." She didn't have to think long. "Helen! She is the only person in this house who would have any reason to withhold any missives from you to me."

"But why? What would make her do such a thing?"

How could she tell him? With her forefinger and thumb, she rubbed the cloth of her dress. She stared at the tip of her shoe that peeked from underneath her dress. "Because—well, because Hans has been visiting us every day."

"Oh."

The distress in his tone spurred her to look him in the face. "He has a legitimate reason since I'm painting his portrait."

"And I venture he takes full advantage of the situation."

"I encourage him as little as I can." She blushed. "I should not have said that."

"You never were one to be coy."

"No, games of that sort never held much fascination for me." She sighed. "I must say, I am quite disappointed in Helen. I knew she favored Hans. I beg your deepest pardon for feeling obligated to tell the truth as I see it."

"I would not encourage you to be anything but honest with me." He rubbed his clean-shaven chin. "I know Helen. She is smitten with that man's popularity and his charm and wit."

"And Luke seems to be making money from his investments with Hans."

"Oh? Has he seen any cash or just reports?"

"I am not privy to that information."

"Of course not." A troubled expression covered Stratford's face. "I was not acting properly to ask you for such information, even if you knew all the facts. I beg your pardon."

"Granted, though apology is not necessary." Suspicion entered her consciousness. "May I ask why you want to know?"

He set his hands in his lap and pursed his lips before answering. "I have disclosed much today. I wonder how many more revelations you care to learn this afternoon."

"I believe our last mistake was not sharing enough news with each other. Perhaps if we had both been more forthcoming, we could have avoided any misunderstandings that have unfortunately occurred between us."

"It would seem all of our misunderstandings were aided and abetted by a family member, mind you."

"She stands accused, not convicted."

"True. All right, then. I will tell you what I know." Suddenly seeming anxious, he stood and paced in no particular pattern around the furniture in the room.

She stood, as well. "Do not delay."

He stopped midstep and looked her full in the face. "I advise you to prepare yourself for some shocking news."

She had just discovered that a relative she had trusted was now under suspicion and that Stratford had a surprising, albeit selfless, reason for paying her debt. Now he wanted to share yet another revelation? She braced herself to learn whatever news he had to tell her, no matter how outrageous or vexing.

She set her heels firmly into the rug. "I am ready to hear whatever it is you have to share with me."

"I am not sure I am prepared to share my revelation, but I know I must." He leaned against the fireplace mantel. "What I have to tell you concerns the man you know as Baron Hans von Lunenburg."

"I cannot say that comes as a shock."

"Then perhaps this will: Baron von Lunenburg is not who you think he is. He is a fraud. He is not even a titled gentleman."

Dorothea had prepared herself, yet the news still came as a jolt. "What? Surely you are joking."

"For everyone's sake, I wish I were. And although by settling your accounts I was able to spare you a considerable amount of embarrassment and heartache, I have not yet been able to do so for my friends. I do not enjoy watching them being played for fools."

"Am I to assume you have no investments with Hans, then?"

"No. He has approached me about the matter many times, but I have always declined."

"So that makes you smarter than your friends," she couldn't resist quipping.

"I do not claim to be smarter. Perhaps less susceptible to flatterers."

"Yes, I have to admit, Hans's penchant for flattery bothered me from the moment I first met him," Dorothea confided. "His words contain just enough truth to be believable, but his compliments are expressed too often to seem sincere."

Stratford left his perch near the mantel and approached her until he drew close enough so she could take in anew his citrus scent. The now-familiar fragrance made her feel safe, knowing she was in such close proximity to a man who would never let harm befall her. "You have always impressed me as a fine judge of character."

She averted her eyes. "Are you sure? I seem to have mis-judged Helen."

"I think not. After all, she may have her faults—and minor ones at that—but she did provide you with a handsome place to stay when you most needed a home."

"Yes, she has been good to me, and in encouraging me to make a match with Hans, she is only thinking of my best interests."

"Yes." His tone indicated that he wasn't sure. "So what do you consider your best interests?"

"Not to pursue Hans, whoever he really is—that is for certain. Just who is he, anyway?"

"Does it really matter to you at this moment? We have so many other things of import to discuss."

She became conscious of her beating heart. "Such as?"

"Such as my declaration to you. My feelings have not moved one inch since we talked the other night."

Dorothea regarded the exceptional curves of his face and the eyes she wanted to look into every day for the rest of her life. She couldn't lie. "And neither have mine. No matter what plans others have for me or what vile emotion might take hold of me in a moment of unjustifiable ire, the love I have for you will not change."

He stared into her face, searching. "How can you be so certain?"

"I–I have said too much."

"No," he protested, "you have said too little. For you see, I must be sure before I. . ." He drew her to him, took her in his arms, and touched her lips with his own. His lips, the lips she had dreamed of kissing so often, even when she was her angriest with him, had finally claimed hers. To her delight, her dreams were but a wisp of imagination in comparison to the reality of his kiss and the love she felt expressed so well in it.

twelve

The clearing of a throat from the vicinity of the doorway across the room brought Dorothea back to the present.

Stratford broke away from her.

"Luke!" A rise of heat flushed her neck and face. She glanced at Stratford, who seemed just as chagrined.

As was proper, Luke pretended he saw nothing. "There you are, Brunswick. I was wondering when you had planned to show yourself for our meeting. I did not even hear the door knocker. Why was I not told of your visit?"

"Do not blame the servants, Luke," Dorothea implored. "I saw Stratford arrive, and I admit I hastened to answer the door myself."

Luke's eyebrows shot up. "I see. Well, then, if you will pardon us, Dorothea, Lord Brunswick and I have important business to discuss."

"Luke wants to consult me about investing in a diamond mine with Baron von Lunenburg," Stratford told her.

Dorothea considered his statement with new understanding. "Oh, I see."

"Really, Brunswick," Luke chastised, "do you really think it is necessary to inform the women about our business affairs? They can offer us nothing in the way of counsel. You know as well as I that finances are the domain of us gentlemen."

"I believe that most women are not as weak-minded as some of us gentlemen like to think." Before Luke could retort, Stratford looked at Dorothea. "I beg your pardon. I hope you will remain nearby in the hope that I may see you again before I depart later this evening."

Unwilling to seem too eager, especially in the presence of Luke, Dorothea simply inclined her head. "By your leave, gentlemen, I shall join Helen by the fire and stitch awhile. I would like to make additional progress on the shawl I am knitting." Though her words implied agreement with Stratford's suggestion, the prospect of withdrawing to create perfect little stitches and watching a skein of white thread turn into a garment of beauty seemed dull in comparison to sharing even the most mundane chore with him.

She wished she could be privy to the men's conversation. Imagine! A diamond mine in faraway Africa. She had heard of mines in Africa, but in light of what she now knew about Hans, she could only hope that the mine in question was not a fraud. Remembering how much money her father had lost gambling, she shuddered.

Forcing her mind onto a more cheerful subject as she made her way to the room where she had last seen Helen, Dorothea wondered what a trip to Africa would be like. She had only seen illustrations of that continent in picture books and heard stories of adventure from her uncle when she was a child. Maybe one day she and Stratford could go on a safari.

What a pleasant dream.

☙

As soon as Dorothea left their presence, Luke pulled Stratford's sleeve. "Come along to my little hideaway, old man. If we want to get in on this lucrative scheme, we must hurry. Lunenburg is scheduled to depart from the parish within the fortnight."

Such a declaration surprised Stratford. The confidence man seemed to be enjoying indulging in rich foods served in fine homes, and judging by the self-possessed tone of his voice when he spoke in front of anyone who would listen, he relished his popularity. So why would he leave in such a short time? Unless he was ready to move on to a new set of unsuspecting victims.

A rush of nerves pulsed through Stratford as he thought about his plan to expose Lunenburg. He and Gilbert had gone over their strategy enough times that they could assure the plot would work.

Meanwhile, Stratford followed Luke into a smallish room on the bottom floor of the east wing of the house. When Luke opened the door for them to enter from the drafty hallway, Stratford noticed the odor of stale tobacco smoke mingled with the smell of burning coal. He had visited Luke there enough times that he knew the space almost as well as he did his own. A man's hideaway it was, with hunting trophies all around and a large stuffed fish positioned over the mantel.

Luke sat in an overstuffed chair in front of the fire. He reached for his humidor made of light-colored wood. "Care for a cigar?" He opened the box and tilted it toward Stratford.

"I don't believe I do, thank you." He decided not to remind his friend that he was not a smoker, especially since Luke was so proud of the fine tobacco he procured.

Luke lit the cigar and inhaled with several short breaths. The tip of the cigar flickered between orange and black as he breathed. After a short moment, when he was satisfied that the tobacco was lit sufficiently, Luke sat back in his chair. Stratford worried that he looked much too comfortable for someone about to embark on an important investment. He inhaled again and took the cigar away from his lips long enough to study the thick stick of tobacco. "This brand of tobacco is one of Lunenburg's favorites. No doubt he will take me up on my offer of a cigar when he arrives soon."

"Yes, he is living well among us, is he not?" Stratford observed as he inhaled the mellow yet pungent aroma of Luke's superior brand of tobacco. "If I were him, I would hesitate to leave the parish, especially in such a hasty manner."

"He has expressed regret upon leaving, but business beckons. And I would not consider his departure hasty," Luke said. "But he does have a reason for leaving at this point in time. You see, his group of investors is in need of a rapid infusion of new funds to continue to finance the miners they have in place. If we can put together enough funds to keep them going another month, we should gain great profits."

"Oh?"

"Indeed. Lunenburg tells me they think they are just a few more weeks from striking diamond ore, and the investment will be returned a hundredfold a short time after that."

"A hundredfold, eh?"

Luke shrugged. "That is what he says, and perhaps he is swelling his rough estimate a bit to lure us. But you know how salesmen talk. One expects them to embellish a tad now and again. If the return on our investment proves to be only ten or twenty percent instead of the amount he proclaims, even you would have to admit that would be a fine profit. And of course the more money one invests, the greater the profit."

"And the more money one invests, the greater the loss should the profit not materialize," Stratford felt obliged to say.

"But it should."

"Luke, your attitude surprises me. You are not known to be a foolish investor. Surely you are aware more so than most men that no speculative mining is guaranteed to pay dividends."

"Of course not. But Lunenburg is so sure the mine will pay us well. Why would a gentleman tell a lie, especially?"

"Why indeed?"

"Besides, he has a considerable amount of his own money invested in the enterprise. He showed us the records himself to prove it." Luke inhaled deeply on his cigar. He rounded his lips and blew rings of smoke into the air. Stratford watched the irregularly shaped circles float, then disintegrate.

"Records can be falsified."

"I would not suggest that to Lunenburg's face if I were you."

Stratford decided to try another tactic. "Let us say he is telling a lie—and I make no accusation now. Of course you know that even a well-intentioned gentleman can make an honest mistake. What if Lunenburg proves to be wrong? I do not want to see my friends lose any more money than they can afford to lose. How much does he want each investor to risk, anyway?"

"At least ten thousand pounds."

Exactly the amount Dorothea needed.

"At that rate, not many investors would be needed for the firm to see quite a bit of money. The miners must be enjoying the equivalent of a Christmas feast every day and sleeping on the finest linens."

Luke chuckled. "The crew is large. They have hired many men in hopes they will be quicker in finding precious stones."

"And you have no qualms about the possibility of losing such a grand amount of money?"

"I have plenty, but I trust Lunenburg."

He couldn't resist a quip. "That is not what Helen seems to think."

Luke took another drag of his cigar. "Oh, are you referring to how she did not seem overly generous with Dorothea when she asked for money?"

"Yes."

"Then it is obvious you are not a married man. You see, Helen does not know the true worth of our family. And likewise, I would hope you would not tell your wife the true extent of your fortune."

"Why not?"

Luke chuckled and set his excess ashes into the ashtray on the side table. "You are naive, my friend. If your wife discovers the exact balance of your accounts and the money involved proves to be even more substantial than she suspected, she is sure to find a way to spend your fortune. And those expenses are likely to be on frivolities such as fancy ball gowns, entertaining to excess, and making extravagant purchases of art to beautify the home and to impress the other landowners of this fine parish."

"As if you wish to live amid squalor."

Luke took a few more puffs and surveyed his surroundings. "Never. And to that end, I allow Helen the money she perceives we can afford to spend on silly notions. But if she thinks she has a hundred pounds, she will buy the most extravagant wallpaper possible for that amount. If she believes she only has twenty, she will find something that serves the purpose just as well—to offer one example." Luke allowed himself a smug smile. "And you have to admit, I would be a poor man if I gave every distant relative who approached me the grand sum of ten thousand pounds."

"Every relation?"

"Ha! If anyone found out I had bestowed such a sum on Dorothea, I would soon discover that Helen and I have many distant relatives in dire need of money."

"So you think she was lying?" Indignation rose in his being.

"No, I do not. But that would not preclude others from developing hard-luck stories that might be embellished to include sympathy, a good dose of guilt, and a request for a healthy sum of money."

Stratford contemplated Luke's attitude. Why was exaggeration tolerated by Lunenburg but not by others? Perhaps because Luke could see a gain for himself in the scheme Lunenburg offered but saw nothing for himself by simply giving a poor relative a sum of money. Such an attitude was not surprising although regrettable. Most men were more concerned about themselves than about others. He recalled stories in scripture: Lot's willingness to choose the best land for himself and the efforts of Jacob's uncle Laban to cheat his nephew came first to his mind.

"Halifax and Crumpton will be joining us shortly," Luke said. "And I'm expecting Lunenburg to offer us all the details about the mine. He has promised to provide a map and in-depth information about his other investors."

"You keep mentioning his other investors. Have they formed a company?"

"No. They are an informal bunch. They are a bit selfish, I must admit. They do not wish to let everyone in on this great opportunity. But their self-interested ways serve us well. We, my friend, have the chance to join in before everyone else finds out about it."

"Hmm." This new information did nothing to comfort Stratford. The mysterious nature of the alliance made finding out more about the other men involved difficult.

"So am I convincing you?"

"I cannot say that you are."

Luke twirled the end of his cigar in the ashtray, although he didn't allow the orange tip to extinguish. "I feel confident that Lunenburg will change your mind."

Before Stratford could answer, the other men, including Lunenburg, arrived for the meeting.

"Ah, I am surprised to see you here, Brunswick," Lunenburg blurted.

Stratford looked for signs of vexation in Lunenburg's expression, but the other man kept his face a blank.

"I should think you would welcome all possible investors," Stratford observed.

"Indeed. I just did not think you were especially interested in the mine."

"Luke asked me to join the meeting, and I do admit I will have to be convinced."

Luke intervened. "I was just telling him I am confident you will change his mind." He stood. "Might I offer you a glass of port?"

"Thank you. I would enjoy a glass of the fine vintage you serve very much." Still, the confidence man looked uncomfortable. "You are welcome to stay, Brunswick, since Luke obviously invited you, but this meeting is meant to be confidential and privy only to serious investors." He took a seat beside Luke, and the other two men sought the comfort of chairs, as well.

The cloak of mystery made Stratford even more determined to remain at the meeting. "I have the money to invest."

"It is not a question of the amount of money in your accounts but of what you intend to do with it."

"Come, Lunenburg, let us not argue any longer," Halifax

prodded. "I do not have all night."

"Relax, old friend." Luke reached for his humidor and offered each man except Stratford a cigar. Lunenburg and Halifax accepted, although Crumpton declined.

Though he felt grateful for the interlude, Stratford glanced at the mantel clock. Where was Gilbert? If he did not arrive soon, he might be too late.

"Indeed, no one here has all night." Lunenburg focused his gaze on Stratford. Puffing on his cigar, he looked down his nose at Stratford. "I will need a firm commitment from all of you by the end of this evening. I have promised the team of investors that I will be sending the funds as quickly as I can. Time is of the essence."

"Such a sense of urgency seems to be a strong tactic when one considers the amount of money you are asking as an investment," Stratford pointed out. "Ten thousand pounds, is it not?"

"Ten thousand pounds? Has not every man in this room lost as much in one night at a gaming hall?" Lunenburg quipped.

The other men broke out into laughter, but Stratford remained silent. He already felt like an outsider; no need to remind the others that, having witnessed many a gentleman come to financial distress as a result of gaming habits, he had developed a disapproval of such places.

The laughter gave Lunenburg the confidence to turn boastful. "There is such a hefty profit to be gained. I promise you, within a matter of weeks, you will all be thanking me."

"Just how much do you anticipate we will gain?" Luke asked.

"I estimate at least a doubling of your investment, if not tripling."

Sparks seemed to fill the room as the men's excitement grew.

Stratford intervened. "I was told you would be presenting a plan and all the details of the enterprise."

"Yes." For a man supposedly prepared to convince others to invest with him, Lunenburg seemed grumpy about the prospect. Nevertheless, he set his cigar down in a nearby ashtray and reached into a black leather valise he had brought along with him. He pulled out a stack of papers. "Our men are working night and day. Here is a list of our expenses."

Stratford looked at the list and then passed the paper to the others. Indeed, Lunenburg had put together a convincing plan. If the company was real, it should be turning a nice profit soon. No wonder his friends, smart even as they all were, had been fooled. If Stratford hadn't known better, he might have been taking a second look at the prospect himself.

"So what do you say?" Lunenburg looked at each man. "Are you ready to go in with me?"

"And just how much money of your own do you have committed to this enterprise?" Stratford wondered aloud.

Where is Gilbert? his mind screamed.

"I have invested fifty thousand pounds of my own fortune," Lunenburg proclaimed.

"Well, you must think the venture will pay handsome dividends," Crumpton said.

"If I did not, gentlemen, I would not ask you to invest along with me."

"Might we be allowed to invest even more, then?" Halifax wanted to know.

"If only I could allow it. But my partners have asked me to limit the amount that others might invest. I have tried and tried to convince them otherwise, especially to make allowances for my personal friends, but they refuse to budge. I am so sorry, gentlemen." He lifted a forefinger. "Although, perhaps once you make the initial investment, I might try again."

"I am more than ready to issue a bank draft. Shall I write it to your company?"

"No, just my name. I am sure we will soon establish a formal alliance, but for now, we are operating as individuals."

"And just who are the other individuals?" Stratford asked.

Lunenburg didn't pause. "Their names must be kept confidential for the moment."

"And no wonder."

A voice interrupted from near the doorway. "Good evening, gentlemen."

They turned to see Gilbert.

thirteen

Stratford breathed an inward sigh of relief when Gilbert interrupted the meeting. *Praise the Lord! Finally!*

Luke rose from his seat. "I beg your pardon. This is a private meeting."

The butler entered, exhaling with a bit of effort. "I beg your forgiveness, sir, but this man refused to wait for your meeting to end. He rushed here before I could catch up with him and inform him you were not to be disturbed. I am afraid he was given directions by one of the maids so he could find you, sir."

My guess would not be a maid, but Dorothea. Stratford tried not to smile.

"That is quite all right. You are excused."

He bowed. "Yes, sir."

Though he had exercised lenience with the butler, Luke looked none too pleased as he studied Gilbert. "This is a private meeting, Meara."

"I invited him," Stratford said.

Luke folded his arms. "I beg your pardon, but I told you it was a private meeting. For investors only."

"That is precisely why I invited my friend to join us. He has something to contribute to this meeting. Something that will be of great interest to you all." Stratford looked at Lunenburg. Instead of fear or dread, he saw hope in the man's face. Apparently he didn't recognize Gilbert and believed him to be another eager investor. He leaned back in his chair and set his fingertips against his chin. The show could prove to be interesting indeed.

Gilbert stepped forward. "I beg your pardon for the interruption, gentlemen, but I would not have rushed into

133

a private business meeting if what I had to say did not have the potential to impact its outcome. I believe that before the evening draws to a close, you will be glad you granted me an audience." He didn't take a seat but remained standing. "I am wondering how many of you gentlemen had met Baron Hans von Lunenburg before he took up residence in this parish."

Silence filled the room.

"With as fine a title and great wealth as Baron von Lunenburg is purported to possess," Gilbert said, and then set his gaze on the confidence man, "and because of your relative youth and bachelor status, you should have been cornered by every aristocratic mother in town with an eligible daughter to marry."

A round of knowing chuckles floated into the air, joining the growing cloud of grayish white tobacco smoke. Lunenburg squirmed.

"Indeed, I do know firsthand the horrors of being singled out by wily matrons eager to match you with their daughters, some less, shall we say—appealing—than others?" Lunenburg assured them.

Since every man in the room had been in that situation at one time or another, an appreciative round of laughter ensued.

Their chuckles seemed to soothe the conniver. "Why do you ask?"

Gilbert wasn't at a loss for an answer. "I ask because apparently no one has ever before seen you. This is in spite of the fact that most of the men in this room, I would venture to say, are quite well traveled."

"Indeed," Halifax boasted.

"Then does it not seem likely that someone would have encountered you at a party, a dinner, a Christmas feast, or aboard ship or train at some point in time?"

"I have been rather reclusive, as you know."

"Yes, that is the rumor," Gilbert admitted. "But judging from what I have learned secondhand and what I have witnessed since my arrival here, you never turn down a dinner or party invitation. So why the sudden change?"

"Perhaps our ladies out here in the country are much more charming than those in London," Halifax offered.

"Hear, hear!" Crumpton agreed.

"Yes, your ladies are charming indeed." Lunenburg let his gaze flicker on Stratford, who cringed with the realization that Dorothea was never far from the schemer's mind.

Lunenburg puffed out his chest. The opportunity for flattery seemed to fortify him. "But Meara leaves out an important reason for my absences. You see, I have been traveling extensively to set up my business in Africa. Though I possess many talents, regrettably the ability to appear in Africa, London, and the Continent simultaneously is not one of them."

"Touché." Gilbert's manner of speaking, practiced often in the courtroom, remained glib among the chuckles of the others. "So tell me, how is your business progressing?"

The smile vanished from Lunenburg's countenance. "As I was telling these gentlemen before you so rudely interrupted us, very well. I expect the workers to reach the ore within the month."

Gilbert crossed his arms and stared straight at Lunenburg. "And just where is this mine?"

"If only I had a diagram so I could show you." Lunenburg took a sip of port.

"I thought you planned to bring us a map," Stratford said.

"Never mind." Luke rose. "I believe I have a current one here. I refer to it often to plan trips." He retrieved a piece of rolled-up paper from a table drawer. Stratford could feel the crackle of anticipation as he watched Luke unroll the paper and study it. "Ah, yes. This is the one." He handed the drawing to Lunenburg. "Now, show us where the mine is, and put this man's mind to rest."

"Yes, do," Crumpton encouraged. "I was curious myself as to the exact location."

"But gentlemen, this meeting is confidential, and not everyone in this room has agreed to become my investor. Suppose one of us should leave tonight and pass on this valuable information to someone unscrupulous and beat us in our own game." He eyed Stratford.

"Since you believe yourself to be so close to discovery, I think we can risk it," Luke said. "Besides, I am willing to vouch for Brunswick."

"And I, in turn, vouch for Gilbert," Stratford assured them.

"Are the rest of you agreeable?" Luke asked.

Halifax didn't hesitate to offer his opinion. "Your word is your bond with me."

"As it is with me." Crumpton exhaled a stream of cigar smoke.

"If you insist." Lunenburg eyed the map a moment before settling his index finger on a spot. "There. This is the vicinity of the mine."

The men looked at the map.

"There?" Crumpton said. "But that is nowhere near Cape Town. I thought the southernmost region of Africa was the location of the mine."

Lunenburg picked up his glass of port and drained the burgundy liquid. "I gave that location initially to throw off curiosity seekers. Everyone knows of the mines in southern Africa. Only serious investors are privy to the correct information."

"In this day and age, such deception is no doubt wise," Luke said. "Based on the figures and other information you have provided us, I am still more than willing to invest."

Stratford couldn't believe what he was hearing. Had Luke's greed expanded to the point that he was willing to throw in his lot with a professed liar?

"So you are more than willing to invest," Gilbert said without missing a beat. "More than willing to invest with whom?"

"With whom?" Halifax asked.

Stratford watched the other men regard Gilbert with their mouths open, not unlike one might look at a candidate for admission to Bedlam.

Crumpton answered. "Why, with Lunenburg, of course."

"So you are willing to invest your money with Baron Hans von Lunenburg."

"Yes." Luke crossed his arms and exhaled. "Come on, man, what is this about?"

"What if I were to tell you that the man you know as Baron Hans von Lunenburg had a very good reason for not attending any society events of which we were aware last season—or the five seasons before that?"

"He has already explained himself to my satisfaction, and I venture the satisfaction of the others in this room," Halifax answered. "As he said, he has been spending the bulk of his time in the wilds of Africa."

"Hmm. Interesting." Gilbert regarded Lunenburg with an unflinching eye. "Tell me, how do you like life in Africa?"

He shrugged. "Life there has its moments, I suppose."

"And the countryside there?"

Lunenburg stalled. "Uh, it is pretty."

"Pretty?" Crumpton asked. "Why, Africa has some of the most beautiful country in the world. Everyone who goes there remarks about it. One cannot help but rave over such wonder and beauty. God's creation unspoiled. Skies the color of a robin's egg, water blue as sapphires rushing against the rocks. And the hunting! You have not seen Africa unless you have been on a hunting expedition. I have the elephant trophy in my den to prove it."

"If only I could have found the time to enjoy such an expedition," Lunenburg lamented.

"Yes, it is difficult to find time for hunting when one is locked in Newgate," Gilbert pointed out.

"What?" Luke gasped.

Except for that expression of surprise, silence enveloped the room. Stratford watched Lunenburg allow the ashes from the tip of his cigar to fall to the floor.

Halifax was the first to regain his composure. "Newgate? I beg your pardon?"

"You heard me correctly." Gilbert pointed to Lunenburg. "This man has not been in Africa setting up a business as he has told you. In fact, as the answers to Crumpton's inquiries would lead us to believe, I doubt he has ever been to Africa at all."

"This is all too much," Crumpton said. "Newgate? Is this true? Did you serve time for a crime?"

"This is preposterous. I think you should think carefully before slandering a man," Lunenburg said to Gilbert.

"As a solicitor, I agree. I am fully aware of the dangers of slander. In fact, I have won many a defamation case based on one fact and one fact alone," Gilbert said. "That the statements made were true."

"And I believe Gilbert Meara speaks the truth," Stratford said. "In fact, I went with him to London to discover the facts for myself."

"London? What did you hope to find there?" Lunenburg asked, still putting on a show of confidence.

"Perhaps you can tell me." Stratford crossed his arms and faced Lunenburg.

"Everyone in this room knows that you are jealous of the time I spend with Lady Dorothea," Lunenburg countered.

"Any personal dispute I may or may not have with you does not alter the facts of the matter," Stratford said.

"I have to agree," Crumpton said.

"And obviously you have reason to believe that you speak the truth." Halifax turned to Lunenburg. "Is this true? Did you serve time in prison?"

Lunenburg cut his glance to each man. Stratford could almost see the cogs turning in his mind as he debated with himself over whether or not to confess. He twisted the end of his cigar in the ashtray, this time putting out the fire. "Yes, only a short time. I was innocent, and everything was all a misunderstanding. I am sorry now that I did not tell you sooner. All of you here are gentlemen of honor. Surely you know the importance of giving an innocent man a second chance. I throw myself upon your mercy in asking you to extend me that consideration."

The room remained silent until Luke spoke. "I believe that a gentleman should not have to suffer undue punishment over a misunderstanding."

The others murmured in apparent agreement.

Stratford felt compelled to speak. "I believe in the power of forgiveness, as well, gentlemen. But there is more."

"More?" Halifax asked.

"Yes." Stratford looked Lunenburg hard in the eyes. "Does the name Clayton Forsythe mean anything to you?"

Apparently expecting to be asked, Lunenburg steeled himself and returned Stratford's gaze with the conviction of a wronged man. "No."

"So you say. I can hardly blame you for wanting to forget that name."

"Who is Clayton Forsythe?" Luke prodded.

Stratford motioned to Lunenburg. "Gentlemen, allow me to introduce you to Clayton Forsythe."

Gasps of dismay and surprise filled the room.

"He has served his time for petty thievery," Gilbert said. "But judging from his latest escapades, he learned in Newgate how to succeed as a confidence man. I only hope that you, gentlemen, will not allow yourselves to become his next victims."

"And how do you know this?" Halifax asked.

"I was on a case in London when I saw him in shackles and in the custody of the law," Gilbert explained. "Of course, he looks considerably better now than he did then. But I still recognized him as being the same man."

"Clearly, gentlemen, this is a case of mistaken identity," Lunenburg said.

"Then does the name Sir Gavin Powell mean anything to you?" Gilbert asked.

Lunenburg didn't miss a beat. "He is one of my dear friends."

"Dear friend, indeed," Gilbert scoffed. "He is no friend of yours. He is one of your victims. One you impersonated." He turned to the other men. "And if you are not careful, he may decide to impersonate one of you when he moves on to his next plan."

Murmurs filled the room.

The cheat's voice overrode the others. "And what proof do you offer?"

Gilbert looked him in the eye. "I admit you were lucky last time. You wisely took Sir Powell up on his offer not to press charges if you left town. Which placed you here."

Despite being confronted with the truth, Lunenburg didn't flinch. "As I said, you have no proof." He let out a victim's sigh, then turned his attention to the prospective investors. "I do not doubt for an instant that your friends are trying to do you a favor. And indeed, if I were seen to be in financial peril, I would hope that you would all be so kind as to try to rescue me. But I assure you, I am not this criminal called Clayton Forsythe. I have never in my life heard such a name. If this ridiculous charge had come from any other source, I would be tempted to press charges myself. But since I consider Brunswick a friend despite our friendly rivalry, and because he vouches for Meara, and because I know they are acting rashly only in a sincere though misguided effort to protect their friends, I am willing to overlook this unfortunate outburst. So if you will write your bank drafts, I can deliver them promptly to my partners."

Stratford clenched his teeth underneath a closed mouth. With an astounding twist of words, Forsythe had managed to travel from the accused to the wronged and had even topped off his speech with a plea for money! Stratford had to admit Clayton Forsythe had learned the tactics of persuasion well.

Thankfully, Gilbert was an equally skilled solicitor. "These partners you persist in mentioning—just who are they?"

"They are my colleagues in Africa," he responded without missing a beat.

"Then they are not residents of London?"

"No. They live and work in Africa. One of them is Dutch."

"So you say. How convenient. With such identities, discovering who they are and speaking to them as well about this investment is almost impossible for us here."

"I do not think I like what you are trying to imply."

"And I do not think you will be receiving any investments this evening, Forsythe," Stratford said.

He stiffened. "How dare you address me by that false name. I realize that you are taking this issue of our mutual pursuit of Lady Dorothea seriously. Too seriously. And now that I am in a winning position with her, you are resorting to the only trick you have left. To dishonor my good name."

"Nothing could be further from the truth," Stratford protested. "I have no need to rid myself of you to gain her affections. They are already mine."

Lunenburg looked at him through narrowed eyes. "I doubt it."

Stratford looked at the others. "You see, Clayton Forsythe is more threatened by me than I am by him. I assure you, my motives for exposing him are pure. My regard for Lady Witherspoon has nothing to do with this meeting."

"I do not believe it," Lunenburg said. "You are envious of me and my popularity, and you would like to see me go back to Africa indefinitely, I am sure."

"Whether you believe me is not the issue. Rather, the issue is how your potential investors feel." Stratford swept his gaze over the men. "I do recommend that all of you wait—at least overnight—before writing bank drafts to this man. He has already told you he will not be departing before the fortnight is through, and so you have plenty of time yet to make your final decision."

"I agree," Crumpton said.

Luke and Halifax nodded.

"Indeed, I have no plans to leave before the fortnight is through, but I urge you not to delay more than twenty-four hours," Lunenburg warned. "We need the money soon, and I have plenty of other investors who would be eager to take your place."

"And as long as they live in this parish, those eager investors of whom you speak are also my friends, so do not think that you can take advantage of them, either," Stratford told him, warning coloring his voice. Feeling testy, Stratford knew he had to leave before he said something he would later regret. "Gilbert and I will be departing now. We can see ourselves to the door."

fourteen

Even though she had been excluded from the men's discussion and had been knitting with Helen, Dorothea did not want to risk missing Stratford as he departed, so she made an excuse and waited in the drawing room. She tried to knit but couldn't concentrate on her stitches. What was happening in the meeting? When he had left her presence earlier, Stratford had looked so solemn, as if he planned to view a corpse and comfort a grieving family. Dorothea understood that the meeting was about the business of investing money in some sort of concern in Africa. She thought that was how men increased their fortunes. Stratford's gloominess worried her.

She heard the muted sound of footsteps making contact with the hall rug. She had hoped they would belong to Stratford, but were two men approaching? Fighting desire to see Stratford and curiosity, she remained in her seat. Instead, she paused in her knitting and took a moment to study her progress.

"Dorothea." Stratford was standing in the doorway. "Am I disturbing you?"

"No, not at all. Is the meeting over?"

"Yes."

"Then will you come and sit awhile?" She set her knitting aside.

As he strode over toward her and took a seat beside her, the faint smell of citrus overwhelmed by the rank odor of cigar smoke wafted her way. Stratford was no smoker, so no doubt he had been in a meeting with the other men. The fragrances entangled themselves in the light scent of the lit beeswax candle burning nearby. Dorothea noticed that Stratford's friend had made progress toward the front door and was peering out its fan-shaped window.

"I can only stay a moment." Stratford tilted his head toward his waiting companion. "I believe we accomplished our mission."

"Your mission?"

"Yes. To keep my friends from making an unwise investment." He smiled. "But that does not concern you. You are my bright spot in all this confusion."

She smiled at the compliment. "But all is well now?"

"Not entirely." He squeezed her hands. "I wish I could spend more time here with you, my dear, but I must depart. I have urgent business that must be concluded, and my friend awaits."

"I understand."

"I will see you again as soon as I can."

She nodded. If only they could share another kiss! But Gilbert Meara continued to stare out the window, shifting his weight from one foot to the other. Clearly he was tolerating their brief encounter so the men could leave and pursue whatever it was that needed pursuing. She couldn't beg Stratford to tarry. She took comfort in the fact that she had been able to see him, to touch his hands, if only for a moment that was all too short.

~

As soon as the front door shut behind them and Stratford knew no one could overhear, he revealed his real feelings to Gilbert. "Something must be done before half the parish is victimized by this imposter."

"Yes, but what? We did all we could to venture into a meeting and make such bold declarations." Gilbert stepped into the carriage.

Stratford followed him inside and sat across from his companion. "Do you think anyone believed me?"

"I think they are torn between their greed, which makes them want to believe Clayton, and their trust of you."

"Greed is a powerful force. It can make one lose sight of the truth."

"Yes, although I think you placed a reasonable amount of doubt in their minds as to whether or not they should pursue the investment." Gilbert tapped his fingertips on his knee. "I must say, your entanglement with Lady Witherspoon has not helped your cause. I think Forsythe managed to use her to convince them that you have a chink in your armor. But if they all decide not to believe you thanks to his argument, it will not be the first time a beautiful woman has come between men and their common sense."

"I cannot control the actions of my friends. I do not regret my involvement with Dorothea in the least."

"Now, now, do not be so defensive, friend. I was just making an observation."

Stratford realized his nerves had taken a beating that night, so perhaps he had been too sharp with Gilbert. "I beg your pardon. I did not mean to be disagreeable. If anything, I owe you my deepest thanks. Your performance in the meeting tonight was superb. If we had been in a court of law, you would have won handily."

"So you say. But as you saw by the men's less than enthusiastic reaction to our arguments, juries can be tough when they are partial to a certain party." Gilbert sighed. "I can see why they are hesitant to disbelieve Clayton. I was shocked by how well he had learned his new trade. His speech was smooth as glass."

"Yes, he has climbed the ladder of crookedness with considerable skill, apparently. But I wonder how he stole from unsuspecting victims before he took on this new tactic."

"Easily. He was nothing more than a common beggar and pickpocket," Gilbert reminded him.

"Then he must have learned how to develop schemes from other cheats he met in prison or from socializing among the criminal element upon his release. No doubt this new enterprise is much more profitable—and pleasant since he now travels among privileged circles."

"True," Gilbert said. "But some time elapsed before he

started taking on new identities. I wonder if he could have taken a job as a servant in a fine home and observed their customs and manners."

"That deduction is as good as any. Whatever course he took, clearly he has expended a great amount of effort to learn how to portray himself as a member of the aristocracy. In fact, I can see why he had everyone fooled. When we first met, I even held a favorable opinion of him."

"This is why we are having trouble convincing the others not to invest with him," Gilbert observed. "That and the fact that he is impersonating a foreign member of the aristocracy, meaning that attempts to trace his lineage would be difficult if not futile."

"But I agree with you that we managed to place a considerable amount of doubt in their minds," Stratford said. "Enough to keep them from investing this evening. That is a start."

"A start only. Now we must convince them not to follow through at all."

"I doubt Crumpton will. He is careful with his money. Which is why he has so much of it."

Gilbert chuckled.

"But Luke is more of a risk taker," Stratford observed. "For Dorothea's sake if for no other reason, I feel obligated to show him the facts in such a way that he cannot argue them. But how?"

"There is only one way. We must reveal the entire truth to the real Baron Hans von Lunenburg. Perhaps if he learns that someone else is posing as him, he will realize he needs to make the journey out here to meet his imposter."

"Time is short. We must act right away."

As soon as they were in the manor house, they rushed to Stratford's study. He retrieved his stationery, pen, and ink from his desk and sat down to compose a letter. Gilbert looked over his shoulder.

Dear Baron von Lunenburg,

Good morning. We trust you are well.

Our business with you is urgent. We have reason to believe that a man who has recently moved to our parish may be using your good name and reputation to encourage others to invest in a business with him that we are not positive is legitimate. We feel that a journey here to prove your identity and to put a stop to this matter is justified. Because the man in question knows we suspect him, he is doing all he can to leave the parish as soon as possible with the investors' money. We urge you to make haste. Please do not write us about your plans. We will be expecting you.

Yours,
Stratford Brunswick, Earl of Yorkton
Gilbert Meara, Esq.

Stratford stamped an imprint of his family's coat of arms into the hot wax that sealed the missive.

"There. If that letter does not encourage him to visit, nothing will."

"But will he arrive here in time? Forsythe gave the men only a day to make a decision regarding their investments."

"True, that is not enough time."

"No, and although he assured us he would be staying a fortnight, I am not so sure that he will now that he knows we could expose his game."

"So we must make sure."

"We must play on his weaknesses." Gilbert thought for a moment. "Vanity. He is a proud man."

"Yes, indeed." Stratford snapped his fingers. "I have an idea."

He drew out another sheet of paper and began writing anew.

≈

Dorothea was completing her nightly devotions when her maid knocked on the door of her bedchamber.

"Elsie! It is well past bedtime. Is everything all right?"

Elsie curtsied. "Yes, milady. But this missive just arrived from the Brunswick estate. The boy told me to give it to you immediately. He even told me not to mention a word of it."

The news piqued Dorothea's curiosity. She took the letter from the maid. "Thank you, Elsie. That will be all. Good night."

"Good night, milady."

Elsie hadn't even shut the door before Dorothea ripped into the message. Careful handwriting, the type of certain penmanship she would expect from Stratford, graced the paper. Stratford had just seen her not two hours past. What could be so urgent?

Dearest Dorothea,

I cannot explain myself now, but all will soon become clear. You mentioned to me that you have almost finished the portrait you are painting of Baron von Lunenburg. Would you be so kind as to dawdle over its completion? I need for him to remain here as long as possible. I will explain in due time.

If you can do this, you have my undying gratitude.

You have no need to respond. I trust you will comply with my wishes, for you know I would not ask if the matter were not of the utmost importance.

Please, for both of our sakes, destroy this letter as soon as you read it.

Yours faithfully,
Stratford

Of course she would do whatever Stratford wanted. She rose from her seat, paper in hand, and looked at the fire. She read through the letter once more and stroked the sides of the paper with her left index finger. Never before had Stratford written to her—at least, never before had she received the letters he wrote. And now that he had finally written, she was forced to toss his letter where it would burn and disintegrate into nothingness.

Heavenly Father, I pray there will be many more letters. Letters I can keep and cherish forever.

She flipped the message into the low-burning fire. When the paper hit the wood, a corner caught a flame and it burst open. She watched the orange heat consume the stationery like a hungry wolf, sending her beloved's words into ashes. She tried not to cry.

"Maybe Helen still has some of the letters he sent," she muttered.

The clock on her nightstand told her the hour had barely reached nine in the evening. Helen was sure to be awake. Dorothea donned her robe and grabbed the lit candle on the stand so she could carry it to light her way down the hall. On the way, she had to walk with slow paces so as not to let the flame catch a draft and blow out, leaving her in darkness.

So she would not invade anyone's privacy, Dorothea looked to see if a light shone from the cracks of the door leading to Luke's bedroom. Satisfied that Luke had retired to his own room and Helen remained in hers, she knocked on Helen's door.

"Come in, Leese," Helen instructed.

Helen was sitting up in bed reading a novel. She didn't bother to look up at the visitor she assumed was her maid. "Set the milk on the table."

"Your book must be quite enthralling," Dorothea noticed.

Helen startled and sent her hand to her chest. "It is, but oh, my, Dorothea, what are you doing here? I thought you went to bed long ago."

"I need to speak with you if I may."

Helen glanced at the small clock on her night table. "At this hour? It must be urgent."

"It is." Dorothea cleared her throat. How could she confront her cousin, a woman who had opened her home to her for an indefinite period of time, with the fact that she was a schemer?

"Then tell me what it is."

Where to begin? "It is about Stratford."

"Stratford." Helen's mouth twisted into an unhappy curve. She shut her book and let it rest on her legs, which were concealed by a green brocaded coverlet. "Why is it that whenever his name is mentioned, unpleasantness follows?"

"Do you really dislike him that much?"

"I did not especially like or dislike him until the night he met you. He was just another party guest before, a man I could count on to make my dinner table even and who knew enough about current events and such that his presence added to the festivities. But lately, he has been troublesome. For example, did you know that he disrupted an important business meeting tonight, possibly foiling a shrewd investment Luke was planning to make?"

Dorothea dug her slipper-covered heel into the bare floor. "I. . .uh. . ."

"No. Of course you do not. You only see him as a dashing man who is keeping your life interesting by offering a rival of sorts to Baron von Lunenburg." Helen sighed. "I understand you, Dorothea. Really I do."

"You do?"

"Yes. I was a maiden not so long ago. I know how enthralling it is to witness two men battle over one's affections."

Dorothea studied Helen's attractive face, which wore a wistful look. She could discern that Helen was remembering her own courting days with fondness. "So two suitors battled over you, and Luke won."

"Eventually, although he was not even a participant in this particular match."

"Helen!"

"The men in question lived in Dover."

"Ah. At your parents' town home," she guessed. "So why did you not choose one of them and remain in the city?"

Helen shrugged. "I like the country better, and Luke was the perfect match."

"A love match?"

"I suppose all marriages are based on a type of love. And I have grown to love Luke more as the years have flown by."

"But what if you had been madly in love with one of your

suitors in Dover?" Dorothea asked, mainly to see how Helen would respond. "Would you have let anything stop you from seeing him?"

"My father would have stopped me from seeing anyone who was not a suitable match, if that is what you mean. I do hope, though, that you are not suggesting that I ever would have been inclined to take up with a stable boy or some sort as that."

"Oh my, never. Why would you think I was contemplating anything of the sort? I do honor to my station."

"Never mind." She paused. "Some girls are too romantic for their own good. I did not think you would be using such poor judgment, especially when you owe Baron von Lunenburg such a debt of gratitude."

Dorothea knew that Helen was unaware that Stratford had assumed her debts. Since Stratford had shared the truth with her in confidence, she felt it best not to reveal what she knew. "Is that why you encourage me toward him? You believe I should let him court me based on the gratitude I owe him?"

"No doubt your gratitude can easily turn to love. After all, anyone can see that Baron von Lunenburg is a handsome and charming man. And even more important, he is wealthy. If you choose him, you will never have to worry about money again. And a woman in your situation should appreciate the value of such security," Helen noted. "Would you find it so very hard to love him?"

"Under other circumstances, perhaps not," she admitted. "But I have given my heart to someone else. Someone who has been writing me letters."

"Letters?" Helen's face wore the proper amount of surprise and innocence.

"Yes. Letters that I have not had the privilege of reading. I wonder why that is?" Dorothea studied Helen and absently rubbed her fingertip against the round rim of the brass candlestick she still held.

Helen picked up her book and flipped through the pages,

ostensibly to find her place so she could resume reading her story. "I wonder why."

"Helen, are you going to pretend that you have not hidden Stratford's letters from me?"

"Whatever do you mean?"

"He told me he wrote to me. In fact, he has been writing me every day. Yet I never received his letters. Not a one."

"Really? How appalling. I shall speak to the servants."

"I do not blame the servants, because none of them has reason to hide my correspondence. I beg your pardon, but you do."

She looked up from her book. "Me? Why ever would I want to hide your correspondence?"

"Because you want me to concentrate my attentions on Hans."

She shrugged. "What if I do? That is no secret."

"So you admit it. You hid my letters."

"I admit nothing." Helen set her gaze back on her tome.

"If you will give me any of them—any of them at all, I promise not to be upset with you. I know you have my best interests at heart. All I want is to read what he wrote."

"That is not possible. I am not in possession of any letters."

Dorothea could guess what happened to Stratford's letters. She stared into the dying flames in Helen's fireplace. Anger rose up in her, but she held her emotions in check. "Did you read them before you destroyed them?"

"How could I read a letter that I did not see?"

Dorothea pursed her lips.

"Dorothea, I do not appreciate your tone. I have retired for the night only to have you accuse me of hiding your correspondence. This is most upsetting. I suggest you consider that I have more than repaid your branch of the family anything I might have owed them with the hospitality I have provided you as of late. Now that your debts are paid and you are enjoying a profitable hobby as a painter of portraits, I assume you would have little difficulty setting up housekeeping anew in London or perhaps Dover."

Dorothea was so upset with Helen for trying to interfere in her choice of a suitor that she almost threatened to take her suggestion and leave the following morning. But she stopped herself. If she did, she might never again see Stratford. And though she had lost his original letters, perhaps he could be persuaded to write her more. Or even better, tell her in person anything he had to say.

"I beg your pardon," Dorothea finally said. "I am distraught over the matter of Stratford's missing letters. If I jumped to an erroneous conclusion, I am sorry. Good night."

She knew she could never again trust Helen.

fifteen

Dorothea counted the silver utensils to be sure they had set out the proper number for the evening's entertainment. In honor of the departure of Baron von Lunenburg, Helen had planned a gathering and had been working toward its success for more than a week. "This looks like the right number."

"Good." Helen sighed as she thumbed through her best table linens. "I cannot believe Baron von Lunenburg is departing the country so soon. I shall miss him. I wish that I could have had more than a few days' notice when Luke suggested that we host a farewell event for him."

"You can pull together in a week a grand affair that most other hostesses would take a month to accomplish."

"Thank you, but I am not sure that Lady Lydia would agree."

Dorothea shook her head. "The rivalry between the two of you shall never cease."

"Probably not." She inspected a linen napkin to be sure the cloth appeared pristine enough to include with the others. "I am about ready to let our laundress go. She is not as particular about her tasks as Mindy used to be. I do believe that is a lobster bisque stain on this napkin."

"If you let her go, who will do the wash? Am I to assume you will take over the chore then?" Dorothea jested.

"No, but I would like to find someone who does not allow stained linens back into our Sunday best pile." She wrenched her lips and tossed the napkin in a disheveled heap next to the folded linens on the table. "So are you anxious about unveiling the portrait of our guest of honor this evening?"

"The unveiling of any new portrait is always a cause for a degree of nervousness, I suppose, but I feel he will be generous in his assessment of the likeness."

Dorothea knew she had already pleased at least one person—Stratford. As instructed, Dorothea had played on Hans's vanity to detain him, and he had stayed long enough for her to put the finishing touches on his image. She still didn't know why Stratford had asked her to make sure he delayed his departure. She had a feeling there was more to the story than he was ready to reveal to her. She didn't care. All she knew was that if she planned to marry him one day, her vows would include a promise to obey him. If she could not abide by his wishes now, she would not be able to find the will to comply with his requests in the future.

As promised, she had said nothing to anyone. In whom would she confide, anyway? She had enjoyed exchanging pleasantries with new acquaintances in the country and had even developed a fondness for several of the women. But her only close friend and relation in near proximity was Helen, and after learning that her cousin hid her letters from Stratford, Dorothea was in no frame of mind to take Helen into her confidence. When anger threatened to fester, Dorothea reminded herself that she owed Helen a debt of gratitude and that her cousin was a fellow Christian who deserved her love and respect.

"This soiree will be bittersweet," Helen remarked. "I had once hoped that you would have good news for us by now, but I have given up all hope that you will be announcing your intention to become betrothed to Baron von Lunenburg. Unless he is saving his proposal for tonight."

"How you manage to cling to false hope, I do not know, Helen," Dorothea told her. "Surely you realize that even if Hans were to propose tonight, I would decline."

"So you say, but he has been known to change many a mind with his sweet words." She exhaled a resigned sigh with a sound that filled the room. "I hope Baron von Lunenburg does not regret calling in the favor with the judge on your behalf. Considering you came to this house destitute and begging for relief from overwhelming debt, I suppose you could do worse than Lord Brunswick. I only hope he is not expecting a large dowry from you."

Dorothea deliberately lifted her chin in pride in response to the dig, whether intended or not. "Stratford and I have been honest with each other. During our discourses I admitted the plight that brought me here."

"Dorothea! How could you reveal such a disgrace?"

"The disgrace was my father's, not mine. And many a titled woman have overcome far worse."

"Thankfully Lord Brunswick is not known as a gossip. Do not even think of breathing a word to Lady Lydia. She will be sure the Witherspoon name never recovers."

"I feel sorry for any woman who has nothing better to do with her time than to nurse her personal pettiness and jealousies with attempts to darken the reputations of others. But I do understand your meaning, and for your sake, I shall reveal my father's indiscretions to no one else."

"Good." Helen discarded yet another napkin.

Dorothea noticed a spot of tarnish on a fork and set it aside to be touched up with polish. "Because of my honesty, you need not worry. Should Stratford choose to propose marriage, I am sure he expects nothing in the way of financial gain. You know, it is freeing, really, not to have much money. I know no one is interested in me solely because he can enrich his coffers."

"Only someone as impoverished as yourself would make such a statement. But I suppose we all tell ourselves little white lies. And you need not worry, either. For the sake of family pride, Luke will provide you with a reasonable dowry to offer a groom, and I will help you with your wedding trousseau." Helen paused in her work long enough to study Dorothea. "At least your appearance is such that you do not need a large dowry to attract suitors."

"Thank you." Dorothea sighed. Helen would never change. Perhaps that was part of her charm.

❧

Stratford peered out the window of his drawing room. Desperately, he searched for an unfamiliar carriage to pull into the drive, but so far no one had appeared.

"I see you have not given up hope, Stratford," Gilbert remarked as he checked his tie in the hall mirror.

"I refuse."

"I wish I held your optimism. But I think we may as well face facts, Stratford. He is not going to make it here in time."

Stratford looked at the mantel clock. "We have an hour yet."

"I knew we should have asked him to confirm his intentions."

"True. Perhaps he has no intention of coming here at all. One would think that Baron von Lunenburg would want to protect his good name and reputation." Stratford crossed his arms and kept his eyes on the horizon like a sailor watching the sea for an approaching enemy vessel. "Perhaps his reputation is worse than Forsythe's."

"Jest all you like, but I have the distinct feeling that Forsythe would not have chosen someone of less than flawless character to impersonate. After all, he is a confidence man, and he depends on trust to ply his trade."

"At least we have managed to bring his trust into question by our appearance at the last meeting."

"Yes, but this soiree that your friend Lady Helen is hosting tonight is sure to be the culmination of the deal. I have a feeling Forsythe will maintain most of his investors. For some men, the love of money knows no bounds."

"I suppose everyone believes we asked to be included in the meeting thanks to our own greed, but at this point in time, I am willing to risk opinion to do what is good and right," Stratford noted.

"Does Dorothea know all the details?"

"Not yet."

"But she agreed to delay Forsythe."

"Yes, and she did a fine job of buying us a few precious

days. Speaking of time, we have precious little left." Stratford dropped his hands to his side, expressing his feeling of defeat. "I suppose I should get my coat."

"Yes. Let us not tarry. Perhaps we can yet find a way to convince our friends not to enter into such folly."

"Unless we are wrong."

"No. We are not wrong. I am sure of it."

At that moment they heard the sound of a carriage pulling into the drive. Stratford pushed aside the cream-colored draperies that decorated his window and peered outside. "Who can that be? You do not suppose. . ."

"Let us hope the passenger is the real Baron von Lunenburg."

They watched the driver pull the conveyance to a stop, then open the carriage door for its occupant to disembark. After what seemed an inordinate amount of time, a man finally emerged.

"Do you know this man?" Stratford asked.

A triumphant smile crossed Gilbert's features. "Yes. That, my friend, is the real Baron Hans von Lunenburg."

Stratford tried not to let his mouth drop to the tips of his boots. Though dressed in the finest cloth, the portly physique of Baron von Lunenburg didn't do his suit justice. He paused long enough to eye Brunswick Hall through dark-rimmed round spectacles and then nodded in what looked like halfhearted approval. Stratford noticed that little bits of gray hair peeked out from under a stylish hat, and he suspected there was very little more hair atop the baron's head.

"Are you absolutely certain this is the gentleman in question?"

"Absolutely. I met him aboard ship on a journey to Italy. He was a most delightful fellow." Gilbert sent him a sideways glance. "Why would you doubt it?"

"I was expecting someone more. . .more. . ."

"More like Clayton Forsythe?"

Stratford hated to admit that he was right. "I suppose."

"Then Clayton Forsythe is talented indeed. He has you convinced that the fake is better than the real man. From what I understand, our gentleman cut a fine figure in his day and was quite the ladies' man among the powdered-wig set. In fact," Gilbert added, "I watched him succeed in charming more than one lady half his age during our trip."

Stratford had no time to consider such an incredible possibility, for Baron von Lunenburg was already approaching the steps. Since he did not know the man well, Stratford decided to allow him to be announced by the butler.

Within moments, introductions were made, and Baron von Lunenburg's concern became evident.

"As you can imagine, I was extremely distressed to learn that someone else has been posing as me," Baron von Lunenburg told them. "My daughters have been telling me that I must get out and about in society more, and the fact that someone else has apparently been successful in such vile trickery seems to prove their point. I can only hope I am not too late to see that justice is done."

"No, although if you had been delayed by another quarter hour, all might have been lost."

"Please do provide me with the details on this imposter."

The two men complied, and finally Baron von Lunenburg decided that Clayton must have learned about him through a benevolence fund he had begun at his church. "That is the price I pay for allowing my name to be attached to the fund," Baron von Lunenburg lamented.

Stratford bit back a verse that came to mind regarding pride. The man may have been vain, but clearly he did not deserve such a punishment for an attempt to help the poor. Instead, he felt it best to broach the matter at hand. "I wish I had time to offer you refreshment and relaxation, but we must hurry if we plan to stop Clayton Forsythe. First there will be a business meeting, followed by a celebration to bid him farewell.

"I understand, gentlemen. I did not anticipate my visit

with you to be an extended holiday. I must say I am shocked by this development. I do not know how to thank you for the opportunity to stop this thief."

"You are the one who will be the recipient of thanks once our friends discover in no uncertain terms that they should not part with any money to fund any venture involving Clayton Forsythe."

Once at Luke's estate, the men hurried to disembark the carriage. Gilbert headed toward the front door, but Stratford would have none of such a bold entrance. "We must not be introduced by the butler. We must take them by surprise. Remember, they do not know Baron von Lunenburg, and questions about him will arise too soon if we must explain ourselves at the front door."

"True," they agreed.

"Let us go to the side entrance of the east wing. We can enter the ballroom from there. That is where the meeting is taking place."

The three men snuck into the ballroom. Stratford wondered what Clayton Forsythe's reaction would be once he saw the real Baron von Lunenburg.

Forsythe was in the middle of a speech. "So you see, gentlemen, all of us in this room are on the cusp of a unique and rare opportunity, an opportunity known only to a select few. Because the limited partnerships available are numbered, I can only recommend a small number of select gentlemen as investors."

Stratford counted fifteen investors. Most of the new men were friends of those who had been at the smaller meeting where he had confronted Forsythe. Obviously, he had not been convincing in his confrontation.

Thank You, Lord, for allowing the real Baron von Lunenburg to arrive here just in time. I pray You will show my friends the folly of investing their money with this confidence man. But if somehow I am wrong, give me the humility to face up to my mistake and make amends.

For the first time in a long while, Stratford wished he was wrong about Clayton Forsythe. But increasingly, he could see that he was right.

"And so, gentlemen," Forsythe continued, "my partners have agreed that those who were at the first meeting will be allowed to invest the sum of ten thousand pounds each in our enterprise. The outer circle, which are those of you who were invited to this meeting, will be allowed to invest five thousand pounds."

"Is that all?" asked a man Stratford recognized as a merchant. "But what about those of us who would like to invest more?"

"I should say you are lucky."

Vicar Ellington! Is Clayton Forsythe so low that he is willing to take money from one of the local clergy? This is too much!

Stratford couldn't help but allow himself some grudging admiration for a man who was so slick he could get a crowd of respectable and intelligent gentlemen to beg him for the chance to invest a small fortune with him.

But his scam wouldn't last much longer.

Stratford stiffened when he saw Forsythe looking about the room, making brief eye contact with each potential investor. His gaze set on Baron von Lunenburg. Stratford waited for a flicker of recognition, then fear, to enter his eyes.

Neither emotion seemed to register with Forsythe. "Ah, I see three more gentlemen have arrived. Have you changed your mind, Brunswick?"

"We shall see."

"Since you are a friend, I shall still allow you to take part in our deal. But only because you are highly recommended by many of the other gentlemen here."

Questioning mutters flittered through the air, while Luke, Crumpton, and Halifax nodded with knowledge emanating from their demeanor.

"And is the friend you brought with you tonight known to everyone else here?"

"He is known to Gilbert Meara, Esquire, and myself," Stratford answered. "We would be more than happy to vouch for him."

"Then certainly his money is good with me."

"Indeed. But you might not be so happy to see him once he is introduced. Or perhaps I should allow him to introduce himself."

"I shall. I am Baron Hans von Lunenburg."

Shocked silence was followed by choruses of questions and pronouncements of disbelief.

Forsythe brought the crowd to silence. "I beg your pardon, but as some of you are aware, Lord Brunswick and his friend attempted to make the same accusation less than a fortnight ago. I see they are still up to their tricks. I have no idea what their motive is for wanting to bring dishonor upon me, but as you can see, they are quite persistent. Perhaps some of you know that Lord Brunswick and I have been enjoying a friendly rivalry for the attentions of Lady Dorothea Witherspoon. I suspect he might be taking the game of love a bit too far."

"I should say, ruining a man's reputation over the love of a woman is most inappropriate," someone said over the din.

"I agree with that sentiment." Stratford's voice was loud enough to silence the others. "I think most of you in this room know me well enough to realize I would never stoop to conquer. My motive is to protect you—men I consider my friends—from folly."

"Does he fancy himself smarter than we are?" someone asked.

"Indeed not. But I know more about this man than you do. And what I know is not pretty."

"Not pretty?" Forsythe said. "Let me tell you what is not pretty. This man"—he pointed to Baron von Lunenburg—"is the imposter."

"How dare you!" Baron von Lunenburg said.

His challenge didn't deter Forsythe. "Can any of you here

identify this man as Baron Hans von Lunenburg or anyone else?"

They studied the new man, but all seemed to come up short.

"I am not surprised no one here knows me. I have lived most of my life in my native Germany. I have no friends or family relations in this part of the country, so I never have had good reason to journey here. I only have a place to rest my head tonight thanks to the hospitality of Lord Brunswick, whom I only met this evening, and my fond acquaintance, Gilbert Meara. They are the ones who invited me here."

"My, how surprised I am," Forsythe noted with a liberal dose of sarcasm.

"You were counting on no one here knowing me by sight," Baron von Lunenburg noted. "If anyone could have identified you as an imposter, your plan to convince them to invest in a fake mine in Africa would have failed. Is that not correct?"

"Of course not. The mine is anything but fake. It is as real as the nose on my face," Forsythe insisted. "I have no complaint against any of these men. Why would I want to lead them into folly?"

"You may have no complaint against them," Gilbert noted, "but you have no complaint against their money, either."

"Speaking of money," Halifax said, "the man you call an imposter seems to have a good deal of money. If he is nothing but a common criminal, as you continue to insist, where did he find the money to blend in with us?"

"The benevolence fund."

"What do you mean?"

"Gentlemen, one of my dear daughters desired to start a benevolence fund in her church in London. She asked that our family name be attached to it. Now I see that step of pride was a mistake, for it allowed this man to learn about a name he could steal and use—an unblemished name—to gain your trust. Judging from what I have seen and heard, this man financed his devious plan by using money given to him by myself and the good members of my daughter's church in good faith."

He studied Forsythe. "In fact, I am sure this must be what happened. Did any of you not notice how his clothing fits well enough but not as well as it ought? Clearly, he took the suit he is wearing from the clothing closet that was meant to be taken advantage of by only the less fortunate who are honest, not criminals. I will have you to know that my daughter speaks highly of her fellow church members. I know they are fine Christian people, and they would be most astonished and appalled if they were to learn how their donations are being used."

"Surely you are not suggesting that our churches should not be benevolent to the poor," Crumpton asked.

"Of course not. We can only do our best and give our finest to the Lord. I firmly believe that most of our efforts are welcome and appreciated and put to good and proper use by deserving people who need help. As for those who would take advantage of the generosity of the church, well"—Baron von Lunenburg stared meaningfully at Forsythe—"the good Lord in heaven will deal with them."

"What a fine speech. With such accomplished skill at debate, you should be a member of Parliament," Forsythe proclaimed.

"Member of Parliament? He has yet to prove he is even a member of the gentry," someone said.

"I thought that might be an issue. I have proof." He reached into an inner pocket of his suit and withdrew identification papers.

As soon as the first few men saw them, their looks toward Clayton hardened.

"This is all a mistake, I tell you. A mistake." In an instant, his voice had turned from the confident tone of a schemer to the high-pitched plea of schoolboy.

"The mistake," Stratford said, "is the one you made in

using someone else's good name and trust to turn a profit in a fraudulent investment."

Seeing he was trapped, Clayton made a break for an exit.

"Do not let him escape!" Crumpton shouted.

A couple of the men closest to him rushed to subdue Clayton, who was unable even to exit the house. Luke sent for the justice of the peace.

Stratford was glad to be proven right, but the victory was bittersweet. He wished he hadn't had to confront his friends about their lack of judgment, even though they thanked him for saving them from their eagerness to earn a high rate of return on their investments. He accepted their congratulations as they all watched Clayton Forsythe being escorted away.

"Allow me to be among the first to thank you for saving me ten thousand pounds," Luke said to Stratford. "Crow does not a pleasant dish make, but I am willing to partake of its bitter taste for the sake of preserving a good part of my fortune."

"I am only glad I was able to solve the mystery before he ran off with half the parish's money. But I would have preferred that he came to a saving knowledge of the Lord instead." Sincere regret colored Stratford's voice.

"Not everyone is destined to become a Christian, I am afraid," Gilbert noted.

"Gilbert, I hope that you will not choose to remain an unbeliever."

Stratford's friend looked him in the eye. "After witnessing how you conduct your life, how you have the capacity to forgive those who wrong you, how you were willing to put your own reputation at risk to help others, I must admit, I am wavering."

"And let us not forget," Baron von Lunenburg added, "your friend went above and beyond the call of duty to help me, a man he had not even met. From what little I have seen of him, I discern that his motives were pure."

"They were, and I thank you for the compliment," Stratford said.

"You have a friend here, Meara," Baron von Lunenburg said. "I recommend you follow his example and be sure you waver all the way to the foot of the cross."

"I will give the proposition renewed consideration." Gilbert gave him a half nod that didn't commit him entirely, but Stratford could see his friend was nearing the truth.

"I always hate to see a man waste his life. Take Forsythe," Stratford said. "If he had used the obvious wit and charm he possesses for good, he could have made a much better way for himself than a life as a confidence man."

Baron von Lunenburg let out a resigned sigh. "That is exactly the reason I started the benevolence fund. To help people live a better life. Not to abuse the new opportunities a little bit of money could afford them."

"Do not concentrate on the one bad apple," Stratford consoled him. "Think instead of the many people you have helped."

"I will, my boy. You possess wisdom beyond your years."

"The few times I am wise, especially on matters of godliness, I believe I am being used as a vessel by the Holy Spirit."

"I am an old man allowed to repeat myself," Baron von Lunenburg observed. "A fine man you are, indeed, Lord Brunswick."

"Yes. A fine man he is indeed." This compliment was rendered by a familiar female voice.

Stratford turned to her. "Dorothea!"

"I just heard about everything that happened at the meeting. You were so brave to face everyone as you did."

"I could not have done anything without your help."

"You give me too much credit."

"She helped?" Baron von Lunenburg asked.

"Indeed, she did," Stratford said. After he made formal introductions, he launched into an explanation. "Lady

Witherspoon delayed Clayton long enough to assure your arrival before he left with the money. He was sitting for a portrait with her. She is the artist about whom we first wrote to you."

"Ah!" Baron von Lunenburg's eyes lit with appreciation. "I now regret I did not respond to the offer to have my portrait painted by such a beautiful artist."

Dorothea blushed.

"Tell me, my dear, do you have any openings to take on a new commission?" Baron von Lunenburg inquired.

Dorothea's eyes widened. "But you have not seen my work."

"I do not have to. You come highly recommended."

"Of course I can clear my schedule for the real Baron Hans von Lunenburg. It would be an honor for me to paint your portrait."

Stratford sent Gilbert a look and then turned his attention to the baron. "Your reputation as a charmer in your day precedes you. From what I hear, your day is not yet over."

"An old man is allowed the pleasure of a sincere compliment to a lady without fear of reprisal on the part of either party. Is that not correct, Lady Witherspoon?"

Dorothea laughed.

"I am sure if Dorothea feels honored to paint your portrait, her judgment is not misplaced," Helen said. "She possesses much more wisdom than I do when the time to judge a person's character arrives. I must apologize to you, Lord Brunswick. I am afraid I encouraged Dorothea toward Baro—Clayton Forsythe far too much. Indeed, I would be honored to encourage you to court her now, and I hope you will accept my deepest and humblest apology."

"Of course, although there is no need for you to apologize to me. You were only guiding your cousin toward the man who appeared to be charming, wealthy, and popular."

"Not that you are not all of those things—"

"Thank you for your consideration of my feelings,"

Stratford said, "but I am aware that the man you knew as Baron von Lunenburg was undeniably charming to everyone he met. That was his stock in trade, after all."

"Then let us wipe the slate clean," Helen suggested.

He sent Helen a warm smile. "Yes. Let us."

"Oh, Helen," Dorothea said, "I have never been prouder of you than I am at this moment. I know it was not easy for you to make such admissions."

"I see now that I was blinded by the desire for prestige and prominence, whereas you could sense Clayton's character flaws. I shall be more reserved in my judgment in the future."

The women embraced. After they broke away, Helen motioned to the food. "Come, let us eat. There is no reason to let all this food go to waste."

"Even without our guest of honor?" Dorothea jested.

"I suggest that we propose a new guest of honor. Lord Stratford Brunswick."

Dorothea's eyes glistened as she looked into his face. "Indeed."

❧

"Shall we go in the garden?" Stratford asked Dorothea as the crowd thinned later in the evening.

"That would be most agreeable."

He led her by the arm, through the side door, and into the formal gardens on the side of the house. She clutched his arm happily. Now that the imposter among them had been exposed and could no longer interfere, Dorothea knew nothing stood in the way of their happiness.

Since summer was upon them, the garden was at the peak of its glory. They could see roses in bloom and rich green shrubbery sculpted into fascinating shapes such as pyramids and swans. The fresh scent of the plants God created complemented the rose water Dorothea had dabbed behind her ears and wrists earlier that evening.

"Isn't the garden lovely," she remarked as they strolled along the path.

"Not as lovely as you are," he responded. "Come. Let us go to the corner, where we can look at the moon."

She observed the white crescent barely lighting the sky. "Ah, the moon is yet again just past new. Much like another night I remember."

"Yes. The happiest night of my life. But it will be eclipsed tonight if your answer is in the affirmative." He gazed into her eyes.

She became conscious of her beating heart and the warmth of his closeness. "Yes. I am sure that is what my answer will be."

"You do not yet know my question."

"You are right." But she could guess.

He positioned himself on one knee. "Dorothea, when I first saw you in the foyer that night, looking so uncertain and scared, yet so beautiful, I was enraptured by you. That feeling never let go of me. Not ever. And since we have known each other, you have shown me nothing but the utmost devotion. You did not even question me when I asked you to detain Clayton Forsythe. You obeyed me without question."

"And why should I not give my utmost obedience to a man I trust without reservation? I have never trusted a man more than you. Unlike my father who, without meaning to, betrayed me by losing my family's fortune, I know in my heart you will never do anything to bring me misfortune or harm. Your love for me is pure, purer than any love I thought would be possible from any man."

"My heart leaps for joy to hear you say such words. I do not deserve you. But I pray you will do me the great honor of becoming my wife. Will you, Dorothea? Will you accept my proposal of marriage?"

"Without reservation, I accept!"

He rose to his feet and took her in his arms. The kiss they shared was even sweeter than the first, a pledge of the love they would share forever.

Dorothea's journey had begun in desperation. Yet with the

Lord's guidance and protection, the journey had brought her to a destination where love was found, where relationships were repaired and strengthened, and where she knew she would realize God's ultimate purpose for her life.

A Letter To Our Readers

Dear Reader:

In order that we might better contribute to your reading enjoyment, we would appreciate your taking a few minutes to respond to the following questions. We welcome your comments and read each form and letter we receive. When completed, please return to the following:

Fiction Editor
Heartsong Presents
PO Box 719
Uhrichsville, Ohio 44683

1. Did you enjoy reading *Journeys* by Tamela Hancock Murray?
   ❏ Very much! I would like to see more books by this author!
   ❏ Moderately. I would have enjoyed it more if

   _____

   _____

   _____

2. Are you a member of **Heartsong Presents**? ❏ Yes ❏ No
   If no, where did you purchase this book? _____

   _____

3. How would you rate, on a scale from 1 (poor) to 5 (superior), the cover design? _____

4. On a scale from 1 (poor) to 10 (superior), please rate the following elements.

   ____ Heroine   ____ Plot
   ____ Hero   ____ Inspirational theme
   ____ Setting   ____ Secondary characters

5. These characters were special because? _____
_____
_____

6. How has this book inspired your life? _____
_____
_____

7. What settings would you like to see covered in future
   Heartsong Presents books? _____
_____
_____

8. What are some inspirational themes you would like to see
   treated in future books? _____
_____
_____

9. Would you be interested in reading other **Heartsong
   Presents** titles?   ❏ Yes   ❏ No

10. Please check your age range:
    ❏ Under 18   ❏ 18-24
    ❏ 25-34   ❏ 35-45
    ❏ 46-55   ❏ Over 55

Name _____
Occupation _____
Address _____
City, State, Zip_____

Maine

3 stories in 1

*F*ollow the mysterious and un-expected paths of the heart when couples face the challenges of separation in a war-torn country. Will those who are left behind retreat from the battlegrounds of love, or can God's healing allow love to rise from the ashes? Titles by author Carol Mason Parker.

Historical, paperback, 352 pages, 5³/₁₆" x 8"

Presents

Great Inspirational Romance at a Great Price!

Heartsong Presents books are inspirational romances in contemporary and historical settings, designed to give you an enjoyable, spirit-lifting reading experience. You can choose wonderfully written titles from some of today's best authors like Hannah Alexander, Andrea Boeshaar, Yvonne Lehman, Tracie Peterson, and many others.

When ordering quantities less than twelve, above titles are $2.97 each.
Not all titles may be available at time of order.

HEARTSONG PRESENTS

If you love Christian romance...

$10.⁹⁹

You'll love Heartsong Presents' inspiring and faith-filled romances by today's very best Christian authors...DiAnn Mills, Wanda E. Brunstetter, and Yvonne Lehman, to mention a few!

When you join Heartsong Presents, you'll enjoy 4 brand-new mass market, 176-page books—two contemporary and two historical—that will build you up in your faith when you discover God's role in every relationship you read about!

Mass Market 176 Pages

Imagine...four new romances every four weeks—with men and women like you who long to meet the one God has chosen as the love of their lives...all for the low price of $10.99 postpaid.

To join, simply visit www.heartsong presents.com or complete the coupon below and mail it to the address provided.